THE BIG BUY

"When can we get the goods?" Frank wanted to know. "We need them in a hurry."

"Come take a look," Jacques said, opening a closet. It was filled with neatly stacked wooden crates. "Do you want to inspect each weapon?" he asked.

"That won't be necessary now that we have a Reynard guarantee," said Frank. "All we have to do is arrange the details of delivery."

As the Hardys turned to leave, they were stopped in their tracks. The front door came crashing down, smashed off its hinges. In burst a wave of men wearing the uniform of the French police.

Each one had a gun in his hands.

Instinctively, the Hardys turned to run. They found themselves facing another gun, this one in Jacques's hand.

"American stoolies," he said, with a fierce snarl. *"Die!"*

Books in THE HARDY BOYS CASEFILES® Series

Available from ARCHWAY Paperbacks

EVIL, INC.

FRANKLIN W. DIXON

AN ARCHWAY PAPERBACK
Published by POCKET BOOKS
New York   London   Toronto   Sydney   Tokyo

This book is a work of fiction. Names, characters, places, and incidents are either the product of the author's imagination or are used fictitiously. Any resemblance to actual events or locales or persons, living or dead, is entirely coincidental.

AN ARCHWAY PAPERBACK *Original*

An Archway Paperback published by
POCKET BOOKS, a division of Simon & Schuster Inc.
1230 Avenue of the Americas, New York, N.Y. 10020

ISBN: 0-671-67259-2

First Archway Paperback printing April 1987

10 9 8 7 6 5 4 3 2

THE HARDY BOYS, AN ARCHWAY PAPERBACK and
colophon are registered trademarks of Simon & Schuster Inc.

THE HARDY BOYS CASEFILES is a trademark
of Simon & Schuster Inc.

Printed in the U.S.A.

IL 5+

Chapter

1

THE FRENCH POLICE officer kept his eyes on the two teenagers from the moment they sat down at the outdoor café across the street from the Pompidou Center in Paris.

Those two kids spelled trouble. The cop knew their type. *Les punks* was what the French called them. Both of them had spiky hair; one had dyed his jet black, the other bright green. They wore identical black T-shirts emblazoned with the words *The Poison Pens* in brilliant yellow, doubtless some unpleasant rock group. Their battered, skintight black trousers seemed ready to split at the seams. And their scuffed black leather combat boots looked as if they had gone through a couple of wars. A gold earring gleamed on one earlobe of each boy.

What were they waiting for? the cop wondered.

Somebody to mug? Somebody to sell drugs to? He was sure of one thing: the punks were up to no good as they sat waiting and watchful at their table, nursing tiny cups of black coffee. True, one of them looked very interested in any pretty girl who passed by. But when a couple of girls stopped in front of the table, willing to be friendly, the second punk said something sharp to the first, who shrugged a silent apology to the girls. The girls shrugged back and went on their way, leaving the two punks to scan the passing crowd.

The cop wished he could hear their conversation and find out what language they spoke. You couldn't tell kids' nationalities nowadays by their appearance. Teen styles crossed all boundaries, he had decided.

If the cop had been able to hear the two boys, he would have known instantly where they were from.

"Cool it. This is no time to play Casanova," one of them said.

"Aw, come on," the other answered. "So many girls—so little time."

Their voices were as American as apple pie, even if their appearances weren't.

In fact, their voices were the only things about them that even their closest friends back home would have recognized.

"Let's keep our minds on the job," Frank Hardy told his brother.

"Remember what they say about all work and no play," Joe Hardy answered.

"And *you* remember that if we make one wrong move here in Paris," Frank said, "it'll be our last."

Chapter

2

JUST TWO DAYS earlier, Frank Hardy's hair had still been brown, Joe Hardy's had still been blond, and they had still been in America.

They had not, however, been at home in Bayport. They were in lower Manhattan, shopping for a computer circuit board. More specifically, Frank was shopping for it. Joe had come along with him just to look around the city after a month of riding his motorcycle or hitting the beach every day, and going through his black book of girls' telephone numbers for a steady succession of dates.

For Frank, eighteen and a year older than Joe, the summer meant catching up on his reading, doing serious weight and martial-arts training, and dating his girlfriend, Callie Shaw. Then one day a messenger had arrived at their home with a package, and Frank had scheduled a trip to New York City.

The package came from the ultrasecret government agency known as the Network. With it came a message from the Hardys' contact with the Network—the man they knew only as the Gray Man.

The Gray Man's message was short and not very sweet. "This is the computer modem I mentioned to you. But remember, don't call me, I'll call you."

The Hardys had first met the Gray Man at the memorial services for the only girl that Joe Hardy had ever truly loved, Iola Morton, the victim of a terrorist bomb. Frank and Joe were leaving the chapel when the Gray Man appeared, a small, balding man in a gray suit, with grayish hair and gray eyes, and even skin with a gray pallor. He was a man who faded effortlessly into any background and disappeared in any crowd.

The Gray Man was interested in Iola's death— but not nearly as interested as Joe, who was burning with anger and ravenous for revenge. The common goal of catching the killers was enough to put the Hardys and the Gray Man on the same team. In fact, it was probably the only thing that could have done so. During the *Dead on Target* case, the Gray Man had made no secret of the fact that he considered the Hardys a couple of teenage amateurs, while Frank and Joe found the Network pros both too cautious and too head-strong—and accustomed to a brand of violence the Hardys disliked intensely.

Still, working together, they had come out on top against a heavyweight terrorist hit squad, which had made the Gray Man decide—reluctantly—to hook up Frank's computer to the Network's communication system in case the Gray Man ever found another use for the Hardys.

The Hardys accepted the offer of continued contact with the Network because of Joe's hunger for further action against the kind of killers who had taken Iola from him, and because of Frank's deep desire to see deserving bad guys brought to justice. To them, it was worth enduring even as dull and unpredictable a character as the Gray Man if it meant getting a crack at terror in any of its evil forms.

When Frank opened the package from the Network, his instant reaction had been, "Typical. They sent me the modem, but not the interface I need to hook it up to my computer. And to think those guys are watching over national security. Our country's survival has to be due to pure dumb luck."

"Think you should break the news to the Gray Man and have him send the interface?" asked Joe.

"How?" replied Frank. "This modem is the only way we can contact him."

"Well," said Joe, "we'll just have to get one ourselves."

They had taken the train to the city, after telling their father they'd decided on a minivacation in New York. They didn't mention the Gray Man's gift. Fenton Hardy was a retired New York cop who had become a renowned private detective. Frank didn't want to stir up those detective instincts, so he said that he and Joe were taking a couple of days as a final fling before summer ended.

So far, though, it hadn't been much of a fling. Frank had been hitting electronics shops since ten in the morning, with no luck. It was twelve-thirty now, and he couldn't argue when Joe announced, "Let's take a break. I'm starved."

Frank grinned. "And I know the reason why."

"Why?" said Joe.

"Because if we walk just a little farther north, we'll be within striking distance of Katz's Delicatessen," replied Frank.

"Amazing, Holmes," said Joe.

"It's elementary, my dear Watson." Frank sniffed the air. "I can practically smell the corned beef."

Katz's Delicatessen was a huge cafeteria-style restaurant founded in the days when New York's Lower East Side had been peopled by Jewish immigrants. It had survived and continued to flourish when more recent immigrants from Puerto Rico arrived. And it stayed filled with

7

hearty eaters and the delicious scents of food as new faces and new generations discovered the restaurant and neighborhood.

"I wonder if we'll run into the Gray Man here," said Frank as they approached Katz's. The Gray Man had introduced the Hardy boys to the restaurant, taking them there as a modest expression of his less-than-overwhelming gratitude for their help in foiling the terrorist plot. He told them during the meal that Katz's was one of his favorite places to meet his agents. He claimed it was the perfect cover for a secret rendezvous. Frank and Joe suspected, though, that Katz's great corned beef sandwiches had something to do with the Gray Man's fondness for the place.

"I hope we do run into him," said Joe. "Maybe he'd put our meal on his expense account. My stomach tells me that we're going to run up quite a bill." Although an inch shorter than Frank, who was six-feet-one, Joe was broader and slightly huskier than his older brother, and his appetite was sizable.

Suddenly Frank stopped short, in front of the entrance to an alleyway.

"Hey, do you see what I see?"

Joe followed his gaze. "It's him!" he exclaimed. "I don't believe it!"

"Let's go!" cried Frank, dashing into the alley. Joe was right behind him.

The Gray Man was in the alley, but he wasn't alone.

Two big bruisers with their hair cut into pink Mohawks and wearing black leather motorcycle jackets had backed the Gray Man against a brick wall, next to an overflowing garbage can. They were slapping his face to the rhythm of hard rock from a huge boom box resting on the litter-covered ground. One would slap him from the right, then the other would come in from the left, sending the Gray Man's head bobbing like a punching bag. From the look on the thugs' faces, they were having fun.

Their fun ended abruptly. They never knew what hit them.

The Hardys' running footsteps were masked by the blasting music. Vicious chops to the backs of the thugs' necks sent them pitching forward on their faces.

Joe looked down at the thugs at his feet, then turned to Frank. "I've got to admit, you were right to persuade me to take a few karate lessons. That teacher of yours showed me exactly where to hit somebody to put him out like a light."

By now the Gray Man had recovered enough to say, "Frank? Joe? What are you doing here?"

"Saving your neck, as usual," said Joe.

"Maybe you should make us your bodyguards," added Frank. "You sure seem to need some kind of protection."

"Didn't your mother ever tell you not to go down dark alleyways with pink-haired punks in leather jackets?" asked Joe.

The Gray Man looked slightly embarrassed. "I didn't expect this."

"I bet you didn't," said Joe.

"But I do owe you some thanks, I suppose," the Gray Man said grudgingly.

"I think some corned beef sandwiches, french fries, and cream sodas would do nicely," said Joe, his stomach already growling in pleasant anticipation.

"Plus, of course, an explanation," added Frank, who couldn't stand the thought of any unsolved mysteries.

"The food is easy," said the Gray Man, "though I hope you'll restrain your appetite a bit. The last meal I treated you to put me over budget."

"And the explanation?" said Frank.

"It's best to keep you out of this affair," replied the Gray Man. "It's big-time, not for kids."

Joe felt his temper rising. "Just like it would have been best for us to keep out of this alley, right?"

"Let's not argue about it," said the Gray Man firmly. "I'll buy you a meal, and that will be that."

He started to stride decisively out of the alley when Frank said, "Hey, what about these two guys here? We'll have to call the police to haul them away."

The Gray Man cleared his throat. "Let's not

bother. I really don't think it's necessary to in-volve the police."

Frank's eyes narrowed, then a grin appeared on his face. "But as good citizens, we *have* to notify the police—unless, of course, you give us a *full* explanation of why we shouldn't."

The Gray Man opened his mouth to argue. Then he saw the anger on Joe's face and the determination on Frank's, and he said, "Okay, okay. I guess I can trust you. I *have* to trust you. I'll give you your explanation."

"Over corned beef sandwiches," Joe added.

Twenty minutes later, the Hardy boys were listening with their mouths full and their ears wide open as the Gray Man explained. "I was using those two thugs as part of an operation. Among other unpleasant things, they're street-level gun merchants who call themselves the Jackson brothers. I was pretending to be a big buyer—too big for their league. I wanted them to lead me to whoever could fill that kind of order. The plan was working perfectly, until today. They'd had a few too many drinks and decided to rob me of the bankroll I flashed them as a sign of good faith. That's one of the problems with deal-ing with criminals—they're so unreliable."

"Yeah," said Joe, reaching for a dill pickle. "It's so hard to find good help nowadays, espe-cially when you need an honest crook."

"So you're still in the dark about who the big arms dealer is?" asked Frank, getting back to the subject at hand. When Frank scented a mystery, his bloodhound instincts came to life right away.

"Actually, we have a pretty good idea," said the Gray Man. "There's a French firm that calls itself Reynard and Company. Its president is a distinguished Frenchman named Paul Reynard, and the company is supposed to be in the import-export trade. But we suspect that its real business is selling goods and services to every kind of crook around—drug smugglers, bank robbers, terrorists, you name it."

Joe swallowed hard. "Terrorists?" he repeated.

"They're Reynard's biggest customers for guns, bombs, phony passports, even professional killers," said the Gray Man. "Reynard and Company will supply anything for a price. Or at least we think they will. We still need hard evidence. That was why this operation was so important. Those two punks were supposed to lead me to Reynard's representative in this country. After I'd made a few buys, I could start dealing directly with Reynard and get enough on the company to shut it down and lock up the people in charge."

"What about the French police?" said Frank. "I mean, it's their territory."

"They've been notably unsuccessful," answered the Gray Man, a touch of scorn in his voice. "Of course, eventually we would have to inform them of what we found so they could do the actual mopping up. But they simply lack the Network's expertise in handling undercover work like this, not to mention the possibility that Reynard may have infiltrated them."

"And now your operation's off?" asked Joe.

"We're back to square zero," said the Gray Man, shaking his head. "And we were so close. Those punks actually boasted that they had set up a meet with Reynard's man, a fellow named Dupree, at the Hotel Pierre at eight tonight. Then they laughed and said they'd rather party all night with the money they were going to lift off me."

Frank looked at his brother hard. He could see that Joe had something on his mind. Something big enough to make him leave the rest of his second sandwich untouched.

"So Reynard will be able to keep supplying terrorists," Joe said, and then Frank knew what he was thinking. Joe was remembering Iola.

"For the moment, Reynard has slipped out of our grasp," the Gray Man admitted.

"Look, why don't you use us?" Joe asked abruptly.

"*You?*" said the Gray Man.

"Frank and I can pretend to be the gun buyers. We can go to the meet and start getting the goods on Reynard."

The Gray Man chuckled. "You've been reading too many superhero comic books, young man. You'd better leave matters like this to professionals."

"Yeah, professionals like you," said Joe. "You did a great job out in that alley."

The Gray Man flushed. "I think we've talked about this matter enough. I gave you the explanation I promised. Let that be the end of this. If I ever need your services, or you ever have any information that the Network should know, we'll be in touch via that modem I sent you."

"I'm looking for an interface to make it work," Frank said pointedly.

"Yeah, your *professionals* forgot to include one," added Joe.

"Well, I'm sure you'll be able to find the part," said the Gray Man. "You young people are relatively competent in dealing with computers. And there's no need for the modem right now, anyway."

The Gray Man got to his feet, ready to leave.

But before he could go, Joe said, "Look, just in case, do you have a number where we can reach you? You never know what we might stumble on. Frank and I get around."

Frank looked at his brother sharply. Joe's tone was mild, as if he had forgotten his disagreement with the Gray Man. It wasn't like Joe to forget something like that or to give up so fast.

The Gray Man saw nothing strange in Joe's acceptance of his authority, though. He simply

14

said, "There's a temporary number you can use—five-five-five-one-one-one-one—while I'm still in the city. I'll be here for another two weeks. After that I'll be back at headquarters."

"Right," said Joe, committing the number to memory. "And thanks for trusting us with it."

"You kids may be a bit impulsive, but I think you're trustworthy enough," said the Gray Man. "Just don't start thinking you can do things that are better left to older, trained professionals."

The Gray Man turned and walked away. As he was paying the cashier, Joe turned to his brother and said, "Come on. We've got a couple of days. We could do it."

"I hate to admit it," said Frank, "but the odds against us being able to pull off a stunt like you suggested are just too high. If I worked it out on my computer, it would probably come out to be about a million to one." He took a last bite of his sandwich and said, "Speaking of computers, let's get back to our hunt."

Joe shook his head. "Look, Frank, I'm tired of going through all those high-tech treasure houses. I want to check out some sports stores. Let's separate and meet in an hour and a half at Houston Street and Broadway."

"Good enough," said Frank, as he and Joe got to their feet. "See you there."

But an hour and a half later, Frank didn't see his brother.

What he saw was a weird-looking kid with

bright green spiky hair, an earring, and black punk clothes.

"*No*," said Frank, shuddering.

"*Yes*," said Joe. "I found a great barber, and a clothes store right next door. You can get fixed up in half an hour."

"No way," said Frank. "I told you before, it's a crazy scheme, no matter how mad you are at terrorists."

"I'm not getting mad, I'm getting even," replied Joe, his face hard with determination. "If you don't want to go along, then I'll do it alone."

Before Frank could stop him, he turned and headed down the street.

"You'll get yourself killed!" Frank yelled after him.

Joe kept walking.

"All right," Frank shouted. "We'll *both* get ourselves killed."

Chapter

3

"I DON'T BELIEVE it," said Frank.

He was looking in a mirror, and a stranger was looking back at him. The stranger's hair was jet black and spiky, and he wore black pants, combat boots, an earring, and a black T-shirt stenciled with the words *The Poison Pens*.

"Believe me, you look great!" Joe exclaimed.

"This is totally crazy."

"Come on, don't try to kid me," said Joe. "I knew you couldn't resist a caper like this. I could see that eager gleam in your eyes as soon as the Gray Man told us about this Reynard gang."

"I didn't want to wind up being an only child, that's all," said Frank. "No way am I going to get stuck with all the chores around the house. And no way could you have pulled off this masquerade by yourself. It demands a cool head, not a hothead. I can just see you taking a punch at this Reynard guy if he so much as mentions a terrorist bomb."

"Save the lectures for later," said Joe. "Let's pay for your new wardrobe and get going."

After paying for Frank's clothes, they left the secondhand clothing store with their regular clothes in plastic shopping bags. They took a subway uptown to Grand Central Station, where they put the shopping bags in coin-operated lockers.

"We still have a few hours to kill before the meet," said Frank, looking at his watch.

"I know just how to do it," said Joe. "Follow me."

He led Frank out onto Forty-second Street and westward to the Times Square area until they reached a large, dingy movie house. The movie playing there was titled *Punk Peril*.

"We can take a crash audiovisual course in our new roles," said Joe. "Besides, I hear it's a pretty good flick."

When they left the movie theater an hour and a half later, Frank gave his verdict on the film. "The absolute pits."

"Aw, it wasn't so bad," said Joe. "The big fight scene with the heavy-metal music getting louder and louder was kind of interesting."

"Don't hold your breath when Academy Award time rolls around," said Frank. He looked at his watch again. "But now it's time for us to do our own acting jobs, and I've got a hunch we're facing some tough critics. If they pan us, the show is going to be over fast."

They took a taxi to the Hotel Pierre.

"We're here to see Mr. Dupree," Frank told the desk clerk.

If the clerk found anything unusual in their appearance, he didn't show it. It was a point of honor among New Yorkers not to raise an eyebrow over anything short of somebody strolling naked down Fifth Avenue, and maybe not even then.

"Mr. Dupree is expecting you," the clerk replied. "You're to go to his room. It's number seventeen-oh-five."

Frank and Joe rode the elevator up to the seventeenth floor and walked down the elegant corridor until they reached room 1705.

"Eight o'clock on the nose," said Joe, looking at his watch. "Zero hour."

"Here goes nothing," said Frank, knocking on the door.

The door was opened by a large man—a very large man. He was at least six-feet-five and weighed about three hundred pounds.

His piglike eyes looked the Hardys up and down. Then he motioned them inside. The moment they stepped through the doorway, he shut the door and turned the lock. The next moment, an ugly Beretta pistol was in his hand.

"Please excuse Simon for not saying hello,"

said a voice from the doorway of another room in the hotel suite. The voice belonged to a lean, tanned, handsome man of about thirty, wearing an elegantly cut white suit and a black shirt. He spoke fluent English with a slight French accent. "Sad to say, Simon lost the power of speech early in life. He has since learned to make actions speak far louder than words. I suggest you do not start any kind of argument with him."

"It's nice to get such a warm welcome," said Joe sarcastically.

"It's going to be hard to do business if there isn't some mutual trust involved," added Frank gruffly.

"There will be plenty of trust as soon as I see your money," said the man who must have been Mr. Dupree.

"Oh, sure, the *money*," said Joe.

"Right, the money," said Frank.

"You do have it, don't you?" asked Dupree, all politeness fading from his voice, leaving a core of icy suspicion exposed. "I made it quite clear on the phone. I want to see a hundred and fifty thousand dollars in hundred-dollar bills as a sign of good faith before we go any further."

Frank gulped and then grinned. "You've got to be kidding."

"Kidding?" said the man venomously. "Simon will show you how much I am kidding."

But before Dupree could make a motion to

20

Simon, Frank said, "You really thought we'd bring all that loot to meet with a stranger? We're not a couple of amateurs. We want some sign of *your* good faith."

Dupree considered the matter. Then he nodded. "I concede your point. You will not have to have the money delivered until just before we board the plane at JFK."

"Sounds good to me," said Joe. He and Frank exchanged quick glances. Clearly, there was a lot that the two punks had not told the Gray Man, probably because they never intended to go through with the deal.

"Have your people deliver it to you in front of the Air France terminal in one hour," said Dupree. "Then we will proceed to Paris to have you checked out. I hope for your sakes that you can produce the money. If you can't—" Dupree finished the sentence with a slashing gesture across his throat.

"Sure we can," said Joe. "We'll go get it now."

Dupree smiled. "Do you really think I would let you out of my sight now that you have seen me? What kind of fool do you take me for?"

Joe smiled back weakly. "Just testing."

"Yeah," said Frank, producing a sick smile of his own. "We'll make a phone call and set it up."

With a swagger he did not feel, Frank went to the phone and punched out the number that the

Gray Man had given him, praying that there would be an answer.

As the phone rang, he held his breath. Then he let it out with a rush as a voice answered, "Gray here. What's up?"

"It's Frankie boy," Frank said. "Get the one-fifty big ones to the Air France terminal at JFK in an hour. Got it? Otherwise the deal does not go down, and we don't take off. Got it?"

"What the—?" said the Gray Man.

"Good," said Frank, hanging up the phone.

He turned to Dupree. "See, no sweat," he said, feeling the sweat pouring out of every pore.

"It is good that you have such dependable associates," said Dupree.

"The best," agreed Frank.

The brothers exchanged glances again. Their lives were in the Gray Man's hands. It was not a comforting thought.

An hour later, they stood with Dupree and Simon in front of the Air France terminal, their little confidence now gone. Dupree was glancing at his watch. Simon was patting the bulge of his pistol in his jacket pocket. And Frank and Joe were furtively looking for a way out of this no-exit death trap.

Then a taxi rolled up to the curb.

A man in a shabby gray messenger's outfit got out.

He had a stubble of gray whiskers on his face and his gray hair was uncombed.

It took a moment for the Hardys to realize who he was and what the bulging manila envelope he carried was filled with.

It was the Gray Man with the cash.

"There's Sam," Frank said to Dupree.

"Good old dependable Sam," added Joe.

"Get the money from him and let's get going," ordered Dupree.

"I want to see if he has any messages for us from our partners in this deal," said Frank.

"Yeah, we have to talk in private," said Joe, gesturing for the Gray Man not to come any closer. "Not that we don't trust you, but we like to keep some things confidential, just like you do."

"You have exactly five minutes," said Dupree, glancing at his gold watch.

"It won't take long," Frank assured him, and they joined the Gray Man where he was waiting, just out of hearing range of Dupree and Simon.

"Hey, great to see you," whispered Frank. "I knew you'd come through."

The Gray Man's answer came in a hiss of rage. "You *idiots!* What are you doing mixed up in this? I should have left you to the mercies of the Reynard agents. Then I'd never have to worry about you gumming up the works again."

"I knew you'd appreciate our risking our

lives," said Joe. "Gratitude like that makes it all worthwhile."

"But no thanks, please, no applause, no medals," said Frank. "Just give us the dough quick, before that hulk's trigger finger gets itchy." He saw the anger still in the Gray Man's eyes and added quickly, "You do have the dough, don't you?"

"I do, though I couldn't exactly take it out of petty cash," said the Gray Man. "I also have something you kids need even more. A plan to get you out of this jam—unless of course you two boys have any objections."

"Who, *us?*" said Joe.

"Enough wisecracking," said the Gray Man. "Listen closely. When you go through the departure gate, you will be arrested by Network men posing as police who want you for previous crimes. That way we can rescue you without alerting the Reynard agents that they are under surveillance. Got it?"

"Great scheme," said Frank.

"Yeah, can't miss," added Joe.

"I hope for your sakes it doesn't," said the Gray Man. "We cannot endanger our operations against Reynard any further by continuing to save you from your own clumsy intrusion into this matter. I'm afraid you can't even think of turning to the Network for help again. I've received orders to act as if we do not know you. If

24

this plan fails, you will be totally on your own."

"Well, thanks for making that clear," said Frank.

"Right," said Joe. "It makes me feel real warm."

The Gray Man shook his head. "It's out of my hands now. Here," he said, handing them the manila envelope. "And good luck." Then he climbed back into the waiting taxi and sped away.

Rejoining Dupree, Frank extended the envelope to him.

Dupree shook his head. "Keep it. I am not the one you will have to show the money to, and it is better for me if I do not even touch it. My bosses get rather suspicious when large sums of money are involved, and if any of it is missing, I do not want to be the one who takes the blame."

"Nice bosses you have," said Joe.

"You will be able to judge for yourselves when you meet them," said Dupree.

Frank almost felt bad that they wouldn't get to Paris. He would have liked to pursue this Reynard thing further.

Joe felt the same way, only more so. Meeting Dupree and his gunman had brought his craving for vengeance against terrorists to the boiling point, and now cold water was being thrown on it.

Still, both Hardys figured that staying alive had

its advantages. They'd be able to solve mysteries and fight terrorists another day.

"Almost time to board the plane?" Frank asked.

"I hope we're traveling first class," said Joe. "Considering the dough involved, you should spring for the extra fare."

Dupree smiled. "You are traveling better than first class—and you can have anything you want."

"What do you mean?" asked Frank, feeling the first stirring of uneasiness.

"Follow me," replied Dupree.

Exchanging quick, puzzled glances, Frank and Joe followed Dupree down the sidewalk past the entrance to the Air France terminal and to a small door marked Private: Authorized Passengers Only.

Dupree showed an identity card to a guard at the door, and they were let through.

"Much more efficient than lining up with the public at the departure gates," said Dupree. "Have you traveled by private jet before? It is a most enjoyable experience."

"Right," said Joe, with a gulp. "Going through departure gates is for the birds. All those officials. They give me the creeps."

Then Frank clapped his hand to his forehead. "But we forgot our passports. We can't get out of here or into France without them."

"You may have forgotten, but we have not,"

26

said Dupree. He reached into his jacket, pulled out a wad of passports, and flipped through them. "These should match close enough," he said, tossing two to the Hardys.

Dupree was right. The bored-looking inspector at the passport control booth for departing private-plane passengers waved them all through.

Waiting on the runway was a Learjet.

"Climb aboard," said Dupree. "Don't be shy about asking for anything you want. Only the best for our customers. So long now."

"You're not coming?" asked Frank.

"Not as a passenger," replied Dupree. "I'm your pilot. Simon is the co-pilot—to prevent any . . . unpleasantness."

Half an hour later, the jet was flying past the eastern tip of Long Island and out over the Atlantic. The Hardys were sitting alone in the luxurious cabin.

"Well, here we are," said Joe.

"No rescue," said Frank.

"No Network," added Joe.

"No idea what we're going to do when we get to Paris," said Frank.

A stewardess appeared from a galley in the front of the plane.

"Can I get you anything to eat?" she asked.

"I won't say no to that," said Joe. He ordered filet mignon with fries and a Coke.

Frank ordered lobster and a Pepsi.

While the stewardess was getting their orders,

Joe turned to Frank. "This sure beats Katz's Deli," he said.

"I don't know," Frank said bleakly. "It reminds me of those old prison movies."

"What do you mean?" Joe asked.

"You know—the condemned man always gets a great last meal."

Chapter

4

THE ADDRESS OF Reynard and Company's Paris office was the Tour Montparnasse. Even though they were across the city, in a shabby hotel on the other side of the Seine River, Frank and Joe could see the office building sticking out on the horizon of the city like a huge sore thumb.

Joe turned from the fly-specked window. "I say we go directly to those offices."

"Dupree told us to wait when he left us here," Frank said.

"Come on," Joe insisted. "We should take the bull by the horns."

"For once I agree with you," said Frank, rolling off the sagging mattress and getting to his feet. "The sooner we get going, the sooner we can find out exactly what Reynard and Company is up to. That's our only way out of this mess."

"Let's grab a cab right now," said Joe, eager to get moving.

"The train would be faster—and cheaper." Frank jingled the few French coins Dupree had given them. "Besides, the Paris Metro is a lot nicer than the subways back home."

Joe grumbled all the way to the Metro, but when they crossed Paris in ten minutes by traveling underground, he was willing to admit that the Metro was okay. Especially when they emerged into the daylight and saw the streets packed with cars in a gigantic traffic jam that everyone around them seemed to accept as normal, even the shouting drivers.

The elevator that took them fifty floors up to the Reynard offices was high-speed, too. Frank and Joe walked down a hallway until they came to a door with Reynard et Cie—French for Reynard and Company—in gilt letters on it. They opened the door and entered a huge reception area with modern art on the walls and a beautiful receptionist in an expensive dress sitting at a gleaming mahogany desk. The desktop was completely bare except for a vase of flawlessly arranged flowers and a white telephone.

"I can deduce one thing right away," Frank said. "Whatever Reynard and Company is doing, it's doing pretty well."

"I'll say," agreed Joe in a whisper. "Any business that can afford a receptionist like that is doing just fine."

He stood in front of the young woman and gave her his most winning smile. Apparently his bizarre appearance didn't put her off in the least. She smiled back.

Frank sighed. Joe would let a pretty girl sidetrack him anytime, anyplace. At least, he reminded himself, that means the old Joe is back. After Iola's death, he'd wondered if he'd ever see his brother smile like that again. Frank got down to business.

"Pardon me," he said to the girl. *"Parlez-vous anglais?* Do you speak English?"

"But of course," said the girl with barely a trace of an accent. "Everyone at Reynard speaks English, as well as Spanish, German, and Italian, plus a bit of Japanese. International trade is our business. How may I help you?"

"I want to see the boss," said Frank.

"Yeah, take us to your leader," added Joe, giving her another smile.

This time she did not respond. Instead she looked them over carefully from their spiky hair to the toes of their combat boots.

"And what is your business?" she asked, her voice cool and professional.

"It's very confidential," answered Frank. "We'll only reveal it to the man at the top."

"That Reynard guy," said Joe. "What's that dude's first name? Paul. Paul Reynard."

"I'm sorry, but perhaps if you wrote for an appointment, someone in management might find time to see you," replied the receptionist in a voice that indicated the conversation was over.

"Look, this is important," said Frank. "Let me give you an idea of how important."

Frank pulled out the tightly stuffed envelope that the Gray Man had given him. He drew out a thick bundle of large bills and riffled them in front of the receptionist's nose.

The receptionist widened her eyes slightly, and her cheeks flushed. Immediately she picked up the phone, punched out a number, and spoke in unintelligibly low and rapid French.

When she hung up, she looked at the Hardys. "Someone will be out to see you," she said.

"I hope he gets a move on," said Joe. "Time is money. Lots of it."

Reynard and Company apparently felt the same way. Joe had hardly finished speaking when a small man in a trim blue suit stepped into the reception area.

"How can I help you?" he asked with a smile that indicated that the receptionist had told him how thick the bundle of bills was.

"First you can tell us who you are," said Frank, putting a hard, cold, suspicious edge in his voice.

"Charles Duval, in charge of new accounts," the man replied, extending his hand.

Frank and Joe ignored it.

"I told the girl we want to talk to the guy at the top," said Frank.

"Yeah, no small fry," said Joe.

Frank was still holding the envelope stuffed with bills. He jammed it under his arm, and he and his brother made a show of turning to leave the office.

"Wait a moment," Duval said. "You are the Jackson brothers, yes? You are earlier than expected, but I am sure we can help you. Please follow me."

The Hardy boys followed Duval through the door leading to the inner offices. Duval led them first to his office, where he spoke briefly on the telephone. Then he led them down a corridor lined with closed office doors until they reached a large door at the end.

"I will leave you gentlemen here," he said. "Please go through this door. I'm sure you will find what you want. Reynard and Company always does its best to satisfy its clients."

"So this is the office of the big cheese," said Joe, after Duval had left them.

"At last we'll meet Paul Reynard face-to-face," said Frank, turning the door knob.

He swung the door open, and he and his brother stepped through it and found themselves facing not one but three men.

The men sat behind a long conference table in a large office with windows looking out over Paris. They bore a distinct resemblance to each other, like triplets somehow born a few years apart. They had the same massive shoulders under the same pin-striped suits, and their faces had the same gorillalike features under slicked-down, thinning dark hair.

They looked at the Hardys with the same gleaming eyes. Clearly, they, too, had been briefed on the size of the bankroll.

"Allow me to introduce ourselves," said the man in the center. "I am Pierre Reynard. On my left is my brother Yves. And on my right is my brother Maurice."

"Hey, I told the chick at the desk, and then that flunky Duval, that it's the head man we want to see," Frank said, still sounding tough. "What's-his-name."

"Paul Reynard," Joe supplied, on cue.

"Yeah, Paul Reynard," said Frank. "If we don't see him, it's no soap. Joe and me just cut deals with the dude in charge."

"An excellent business principle," said Pierre Reynard, who apparently did the talking for the brothers. "But evidently you don't understand the nature of our business. Our dear uncle Paul may be officially the head of this company, but he prefers to spend his time at his estate in Normandy, where he pursues his passion for breeding horses. His only connection with the company is that he receives his share of the profits. And as long as the profits continue to grow as they have, he is happy to leave Reynard and Company in the hands of us, his nephews."

One of the other brothers, Yves, finally spoke.

His voice was harsher and cruder than Pierre's cultivated tone. "So let's get down to business," he said. "Our time is valuable. What do you want from us? What are you willing to pay?"

"We want as many handguns and assault rifles as one hundred and fifty thousand American dollars will buy," said Frank. "We'd prefer the FN-FAL assault rifle, French manufacture will do, and the NATO-issue Belgian nine-millimeter Browning automatic pistol. Needless to say, they all must have serial numbers that can't be traced."

Frank had read a long article on terrorist weaponry the year before. He was grateful for his accurate memory as he saw the Reynard brothers nod in recognition of the names he had mentioned.

"And exactly what do you plan to do with these weapons?" asked Pierre, after exchanging quick glances with his brothers. "Not that we are saying we can sell them to you," he added.

"Let's just say I have a good use for them," replied Frank. "The less you know, the better it is for everyone."

"And who recommended our firm to you?" asked Pierre, his eyes intently watchful now.

"A friend who would prefer that his name not be revealed," said Frank. "You know how it is with some people. They're shy."

"Look, enough of this chatter," Joe interrupted with a grimace of impatience. "As far as

I'm concerned, money talks—and if you don't want to listen, we'll find somebody who does."

Pierre shrugged and said, "I am very sorry, gentlemen, but somebody gave you what I believe you Americans call 'a bum steer.' Reynard and Company does not engage in the sort of trade you have mentioned. In fact, if not for our tradition of complete business confidentiality, we would be forced to inform the police of your proposition. And in France, the penalty for illegal weapons possession is very harsh indeed."

Frank and Joe looked at the Reynard brothers one by one. Each brother gave the Hardys the same cold stare.

"I believe you gentlemen know the way out," said Pierre in a chilly voice.

"Yeah," replied Joe with disgust. "We're on our way."

Without another word, the Hardys left the office and walked back through the corridor toward the reception area.

"I could have sworn we had them on the hook," said Frank, shaking his head. "I wonder what we did wrong."

They entered the reception area and were heading for the exit when they heard the voice of the receptionist calling after them.

"Gentlemen, would you please leave me your address in Paris in case we should want to be in touch with you?" she asked. Clearly, she had been contacted over the intercom as soon as the Hardys had left the Reynard brothers' office.

Frank gave her the name of the hotel, and she said, "May I suggest you return there immediately."

"I figured we'd have some lunch first," said Joe. "Say, maybe you could tell us a nice place to eat. In fact, why not have lunch with us? You know, make a couple of strangers feel at home."

Her response was simply, "May I suggest you return to your hotel immediately."

"Real French hospitality," muttered Joe, as he and his brother left.

"Don't take it as an insult to your famous way with women," said Frank. "Obviously, she had her orders. Let's get back to the hotel fast. I have a hunch something's waiting for us there."

What was waiting was a telephone message at the desk in the lobby. It was a very short message: a telephone number and the words "Call immediately."

When Frank made the call from their room, the person who answered obviously was expecting to hear from them. Before Frank could say a word, a voice answered the phone in English. "Mr. Jackson?"

"Right," Frank answered.

"You and your brother will be sitting outside at the Café des Nations opposite the Pompidou Center at four this afternoon," the voice said. "You will be contacted by someone who will say to you, 'Brother, can you spare a million?' Is that clear?"

"Yes, but—" Frank said.

There was a click on the other end of the line. Frank turned to Joe.

"I think we're in business," he said.

Three hours later, though, sitting in the summer late-afternoon sunlight at the Café des Nations, Frank was having a hard time keeping Joe's mind on business. He had no sooner made Joe break off a budding friendship with two pretty girls who had stopped in front of their table, when another one appeared. One look at her, and Frank knew that Joe would be hard to discourage.

She looked about eighteen years old. Her pale complexion was flawless and untouched by makeup except for dark shading around her green eyes. Her hair was flaming red, and if it was dyed, it was very well done. She wore a white T-shirt that showed off her slim figure, faded blue jeans that hugged her legs down to her bare ankles, and high-heeled sandals. Joe didn't have to utter a word to say what he thought of her. His eyes said it all: Gorgeous!

Even Frank wasn't exactly eager to get rid of her.

Especially when she leaned toward them, gave

them a smile, and said, "Brother, can you spare a million?"

"Sit down," Joe said instantly.

But the girl remained standing. Her gaze flicked toward the policeman who stood watching them.

"Too hot out here in the sun," she said with the faintest of French accents. "I know someplace that's cooler. Come on."

Frank left some change on the table to pay for the coffees, then he and Joe hurried off with the girl.

"What's your name?" Joe asked.

"Denise," she replied. "And which brother are you, Joe or Frank?"

"I'm Joe," Joe said. "The handsome, charming one."

"Where are we going?" asked Frank.

"And that's Frank," Joe added. "The dull, businesslike one."

"Speaking of business," said Denise, "do you have the money?"

"Do you have the goods?" asked Frank.

"*Trust* the young lady," Joe said, putting his arm around her shoulder. "Anyone who looks as good as she does can't be bad."

"First, you answer," Denise said to Frank.

"I've got the money," said Frank.

"Then I've got the goods," said Denise.

The Hardys and Denise were walking through a

maze of twisting streets behind the Pompidou Center. Denise glanced over her shoulder each time they turned, making sure they weren't being followed. Finally she seemed satisfied.

"In here," she said, indicating the entranceway to a grime-covered old building.

They entered a dark hallway, and Denise flicked a switch.

"We have to hurry up the stairs," she said. "The light stays on for just sixty seconds."

At the top of the creaking stairs was a steel door, which clearly had been installed to discourage thieves. Denise rapped loudly on it: four raps, a pause, and then two more.

The Hardys heard the sound of a bolt being unfastened and then a voice saying, *"Entrez."*

Denise swung the door open and motioned for Frank and Joe to go in first.

They did.

A man was waiting for them in the center of a shabbily furnished room.

Neither Frank nor Joe could have said what he looked like.

All they could see was what was in his hand.

It was a pistol—and it was pointed directly at them.

Chapter
5

FRANK AND JOE froze.

They heard Denise's voice behind them. "That's enough, Jacques. Stop joking."

The man shrugged his shoulders, grinned, and lowered the gun.

The Hardys relaxed. "Jacques has a very crude sense of humor," Denise said.

Jacques grinned and began to chatter away in French.

"Speak English, Jacques," said Denise sharply. "These are important clients."

"Okay, okay. Sorry, guys, just wanted a couple of kicks," said Jacques, with a heavy accent. "No bad feelings, okay?"

"Look, man, I'm not into mixing business with pleasure," said Frank.

"Yeah," agreed Joe. "Not when the business is as serious as this is."

"Jacques was merely giving you a demonstration of the goods," said Denise soothingly.

"Yes, of course," said Jacques, as he extended the pistol, butt end first, toward the Hardys. "Take a closer look."

Frank took the pistol and examined it.

"You'll find that it's what you specified," said Denise. "A NATO-issue Belgian nine millimeter."

"And take a look at *this*," Jacques went on. He picked up a compact, deadly-looking rifle from a table and tossed it to Joe, who caught it and worked the action.

"That is the greatest assault rifle on earth," Jacques said fervently. "Seventy rounds a minute and no jamming."

"Looks fine to me," said Joe.

"Reynard and Company is certainly efficient," Frank added. "Give my congratulations to your bosses. On second thought, I'll do it myself, when we arrange delivery of the full shipment and I make payment."

"Who said anything about Reynard and Company?" said Denise. "Did you hear that name mentioned, Jacques?"

"What name?" replied Jacques, grinning again. "I hear nothing but what I am supposed to hear. Some things are dangerous to hear. Even more dangerous than these guns."

"This time Jacques isn't joking," said Denise. "We are the people you two will be dealing with. You give us the money, and we deliver the goods."

Frank exchanged a quick glance with Joe. Things were taking a wrong turn, possibly heading toward a dead end. He had to get them back on the right track.

"Hey, what do you take us for—suckers?" he asked. "We went to Reynard and Company because they had a good rep. Too good a rep for them to risk damaging it by ripping us off. But there's no way we're going to cut a deal with small fry. What's to stop you from grabbing our dough and offing us?"

"Yeah," said Joe. "Either we get the word from the big boys at Reynard, or we take our business elsewhere."

Denise merely looked thoughtful at the Hardys' response, but Jacques did more than that. His face darkening, he pulled another pistol from his pocket. It was smaller than the first, but it looked just as efficient.

"The weapons you have in your hands have no bullets," he said. "This gun has. Now you will hand over your money."

"Are you crazy?" exclaimed Frank. "You think we brought it with us?"

"That's a real joke," said Joe. "You aren't dealing with amateurs, you know."

"Of course we're not," replied Denise. Once

again her voice was soothing. "I told you once, Jacques, no more jokes. Put your little toy away."

Scowling, Jacques reluctantly put his pistol back in his pocket.

"Good," said Frank, trying to keep the relief out of his voice. "Now let's get back to business. You *are* working for Reynard then?"

"I can see you're too shrewd to try to fool," said Denise, smiling. "You win. We do work for Reynard."

"We'll need proof of that," said Frank.

Joe grinned at Denise. "Yeah, don't think you can just bat your eyes at us and convince us." He paused. "That's not to say they're not real pretty green eyes. In fact—"

"Like I said, we can get back to business now," said Frank. "Proof is what we want."

"And proof is what you'll get," Denise answered. "Please excuse me for a moment."

She disappeared into the next room of the apartment. The Hardys could hear her talking in a low voice over the telephone, but there was no way they could have caught what she said, even if they had understood her rapidly spoken French. Her conversation lasted a full five minutes.

When she returned, she said, "Would you go to the phone, please?"

Frank and Joe, followed by Denise and Jacques, went into the next room. It was a bedroom, as shabbily furnished as the living room. Frank noticed that the mattress on the bed was bare. He suspected that no one actually lived in the apartment.

Denise indicated that he should pick up the phone receiver, which was off the hook. Frank did so, with Joe standing next to him.

"Hello, Mr. Jackson," said a voice Frank recognized. "This is Pierre Reynard. I want to assure you that you can trust Denise and Jacques. Reynard and Company stands behind them."

"And I assume you will give a money-back guarantee if the goods prove unsatisfactory," said Frank.

"Of course, Mr. Jackson," Pierre said. "Reynard and Company takes pride in providing the highest-quality service."

"That's what I wanted to know," said Frank, and hung up.

"Satisfied?" asked Denise.

"Satisfied," said Frank.

"I knew a girl as pretty as you could be trusted," said Joe.

"Flattery will get you everywhere," replied Denise, returning his winning smile.

"When can we inspect the goods?" Frank wanted to know. "We need them in a hurry. You know, pressing business."

"Our customers usually do have pressing business," said Jacques. "We, too, do not like to waste time. Come and take a look."

Jacques opened a bedroom closet. It was filled with neatly stacked wooden crates.

"Do you want to open them and inspect each weapon?" Jacques asked.

"That won't be necessary now that we have a Reynard guarantee," said Frank. "All we have to do is arrange the details of delivery."

As he spoke, Frank's mind was working feverishly. He had wanted things to happen fast, but not this fast. "I'll fill you in on the details tomorrow," he said. "It'll take that long to work things out with the other members of my group. We'll rendezvous here tomorrow, okay?"

But before they could leave, Denise said, "Wait a moment. I have to see what my boss says."

She made another phone call and reported the situation. "He says that you have seen our goods, now we must be able to count your money, or else no deal. *You* can trust Reynard and Company, but *we* have no reason to trust *you* now that you know where the weapons are stored. If you don't mind, we will accompany you back to your hotel room to look at your cash."

"No need to do that," said Frank. He removed the money from his pockets.

"So you had it on you all the time," said Denise admiringly. "Very cool of you."

"Got to be cool in this business," said Joe. "Lose your cool and you're done for."

"It is a pleasure to do business with such professionals." Denise took the money and counted it rapidly, then handed it back to Frank. "I will not even ask to keep it before we make the delivery. I can see that you are too sharp a businessman to agree to that, just as I can be sure that you have too much to lose to try to double-cross us. I will tell the boss you are okay."

She spoke again briefly on the phone, and hung up. Then she turned to Frank and Joe. "Until tomorrow."

"See you," said Frank.

"Look, if you're not doing anything tonight, maybe we can—" Joe began.

"Come on, Joe," Frank said, eager to reach a phone of his own.

"My brother may be a real sharp businessman, but he's also a real wet blanket," Joe said to Denise.

"Come on," Frank repeated, already on his way out.

"Okay, okay," said Joe.

But the Hardys didn't reach the front door before they were stopped in their tracks.

They'd just gotten into the living room when the front door came crashing in, smashed off its hinges.

Through the doorway burst a wave of men,

some in suits, others in the uniforms of the French police.

Each one had a gun in his hands.

Instinctively, the Hardys turned to run.

They found themselves facing another gun, this one in Jacques's hand.

"American stoolies," he said, with a fierce snarl. *"Die!"*

"No!" Frank shouted. "You've got us wrong. We didn't—"

But his denial was blotted out by the roar of a pistol shot.

Chapter

6

FRANK AND JOE turned toward each other, each checking to see if the other had been hit.

Then they saw who the victim was.

The pistol dropped from Jacques's hand as he clutched his chest. He fell forward with a startled expression on his face and lay face downward on the floor, motionless.

Instantly Denise was on her knees beside him. "Filthy beasts!" she screamed at the policeman who seized her.

Meanwhile both Hardys were seized as well, while other cops held pistols on them.

Joe opened his mouth to protest but shut it fast when he remembered that there was no Network standing behind him and Frank. They were on their own, and the evidence identifying them as gun dealers was overwhelming.

Both Frank and Joe kept quiet as their arms were jerked behind them and handcuffs were snapped on their wrists, the cold metal pinching their flesh. Then they and Denise were hustled out of the apartment and down the stairs. But before they opened the door to the street, their captors stopped.

"What the—" Frank exclaimed, as he felt someone behind him slipping something over his head. It was a blindfold.

"Hey, what are you trying to do?" he heard Joe protest. Evidently, Joe was getting the same treatment.

Hands shoved them outside. They heard a door opening, and then they were pushed onto a car seat. The door slammed, a motor roared into life, and they felt the car begin to move.

"Hey, anybody here?" Frank asked.

"I am," replied Joe, on one side of him.

"Me, too," said Denise, on the other.

"What kind of cops would blindfold us like this?" asked Frank, turning toward Denise.

"A very special kind, I'm afraid," Denise whispered, her voice sounding defeated and scared. "They're from the Sûreté—French Intelligence. They deal with only the most serious crimes, and they're allowed to do virtually anything they want in order to combat them."

"But why the blindfolds?" asked Joe. "Those

cops looked too big and tough to be playing kids' games."

"This is no game, unfortunately." Denise struggled to keep her voice from trembling. "The blindfolds mean we are being taken to one of their secret detention centers. Officially, these centers are not supposed to exist. Just as, officially, law enforcement agents are not supposed to do what they do to prisoners there. But how can prisoners later complain or protest about their treatment when they cannot give the locations of these places that do not officially exist?"

"What do they do to prisoners there—or shouldn't I ask?" said Joe.

"You shouldn't ask," replied Denise. "You will find out soon enough, anyway."

The rest of the ride was passed in silence except for the car radio, which was tuned in to a station devoted to American country-and-western music. One of the cops must have been a fan. Frank heard Johnny Cash singing about being stuck in Folsom Prison. He decided that at the moment that didn't sound so bad.

Finally the car stopped. Frank heard Joe say, "Take it easy, man." Then he was pulled out and shoved roughly across a sidewalk and into a building. A door slammed shut behind him, and the blindfold was yanked away.

Frank, Joe, and Denise stood in a room filled with metal office furniture and towering filing cabinets. Six plainclothesmen stood guard. Not one of them was under six feet tall. A small man sat at a metal desk in front of them, a large ledger open on top of it.

Systematically, each of the prisoners was frisked.

The cop frisking Frank grinned when he found the bundles of hundred-dollar bills. He tossed them on the desk. The man on the desk counted the money and made a notation in his ledger.

"Hey, I want a receipt for that," cried Frank, in the voice of an offended citizen demanding his rights.

"Ah, you are an American," the man at the desk said, and gave a small, humorless smile. "You are in luck that we speak your language here. A good number of our prisoners come from abroad."

"I said, I want a receipt. I worked hard for that money," said Frank. "I just came back from a job in the Arabian desert. Send for my passport if you don't believe me."

"So that is your story," said the desk man. "Of course we will give you a receipt. Armand, give the American gentleman a receipt for his hard-earned cash."

The cop beside Frank spun him around, then slammed the back of his hand across Frank's face. Stars erupted in front of Frank's eyes, and he tasted blood. He shook his head, dazed.

"Any more requests?" asked the man at the desk.

"You can't get away with this!" exploded Joe. His muscles strained as he tried futilely to free his handcuffed hands. "I demand to call a lawyer. I know we have that right."

"Ah, you have such a touching faith in your 'rights,' " said the man at the desk. "François, show the American what he has a right to here."

A moment later, Joe, too, was shaking his head after being viciously backhanded.

"Please, don't say anything more," Denise pleaded with them. "These guys are not like the nice cops you see on your television."

"Take the lady's advice," said the man at the desk. "It will save you considerable pain and discomfort—for the moment at least."

"We get the point," replied Frank. He moved his tongue around the inside of his mouth and found with relief that no teeth had been loosened.

"Yeah, okay, we'll be good little boys—for the moment at least," said Joe, unable to mask his anger.

The cop next to Joe raised his hand to deliver another blow, but the man at the desk shook his head.

"Enough," he said. "We want the Americans to be in good shape for their interrogation, otherwise they might pass out too quickly. Take them to their cells while we prepare to question them. I hope they will use the time to see reason and to realize how intelligent it would be to spare themselves additional pain."

53

Frank, Joe, and Denise were taken from the room and led down a stairway.

"Once, long ago," one of the cops said, "this used to be a wine cellar. Now we use it to store prisoners—until we pull their corks."

Frank and Joe were thrust into a windowless cell made of stainless steel. It was ventilated by ducts in the high ceiling.

"We are very proper here. We give men and women separate accommodations," the cop went on. "But don't pine away for your lovely companion here," he added, indicating Denise. "I assure you, you will be seeing one another soon enough."

As soon as the door slammed shut, Joe opened his mouth to speak. But he stopped when Frank shook his head sharply.

Frank put his mouth close to Joe's ear and whispered, "This place has to be bugged. It's probably televised, too. So no talking, just whispering."

"Right." Joe nodded. He thought for a moment, then whispered. "Any ideas about what to do now?"

Frank looked at him for a moment. "I was about to ask you the same thing. Do you think you can bust us out of here?"

"Oh, sure, if you happen to have some dynamite hidden on you somewhere," replied Joe sarcastically.

The Hardys fell silent.

"Maybe we can tell the cops our story," Joe said after several minutes. "How we're really trying to stop Reynard, and—"

"Forget it, Joe," Frank cut in. "It's a wild story to begin with, and there's no one to back us up. You remember what the Gray Man said. On this case, we don't exist anymore as far as the Network is concerned. From here on in, we'll have to wing it and hope we're not riding for a big fall."

At that moment, the door opened, and the Hardys sprang apart.

The little man who had been behind the desk entered accompanied by two scowling cops.

"I see you have been putting your heads together to consider your situation," he said. "I hope you have come to your senses and decided to cooperate with our investigation. As an added inducement, I can promise you immunity from prosecution and a plane ticket out of the country if you reveal what you know about this traffic in illegal weapons."

"Illegal weapons?" said Frank. "What illegal weapons?"

"We were just paying a social call when you guys came busting in," said Joe. "You cops have a lot of nerve. I bet you didn't even have a search warrant. Wait until I see my lawyer."

The little man gave a mock sigh of sadness. "You Americans have so much to learn about the way we do things here. You think crime is some kind of game. We take it more seriously. I hope for your sakes that you learn quickly. Come, you will now have your first lesson."

Frank and Joe were led out of their steel cell and pushed roughly down a corridor to another, larger steel room. It contained only one piece of furniture—a chair with metal bands designed to fasten a person's arms to the armrests. Next to the chair stood a tall man with a huge stomach and a shaven skull. In one corner stood Denise, a cop guarding her. Her handcuffs had been taken off, but she didn't look as if she was about to make any moves. She was pale and trembled slightly.

"You see, your girlfriend here already knows what this chair is for," said the little man. "It is quite an ingenious piece of equipment. And very effective. I like to call it our truth machine."

The man who stood beside the chair flashed an ugly grin. Most of his teeth were made of steel.

"Karl here is the finest operator of the truth machine that we have," the little man said. The small man's teeth were all his own, but his smile wasn't any prettier. "He has been operating it ever since it was made for a little war we had in Algeria, about thirty years ago. Karl was in our Foreign Legion then. We don't ask what he did before that. The Sûreté has found considerable use for his skills. But enough talk. I am sure Karl is eager to demonstrate to foreign visitors how his machine works. Which one of you Americans wants to have the first lesson?''

"Me," said Frank.

"No, me," said Joe.

"You were the first to speak," the little man said to Frank. "So you will be the lucky one."

Frank's handcuffs were taken off. He was shoved into the chair, and the metal bands were snapped around his forearms and wrists.

"Henri and François, you may leave now," the little man said. "Remember to close the door tightly behind you."

After the two cops left, leaving the little man, Karl, and one other cop to take care of the prisoners, the little man explained, "Some of our men don't enjoy watching the truth machine in operation. In fact, we have even made this room totally soundproof to spare the more delicate feelings among us. The screams can become ear-splittingly loud at times."

Then he said to Karl, *"Commencez."*

Karl stopped grinning but continued to smile softly to himself as he set to work. He opened a small kit and took out some long wires, which he ran from electric outlets in the wall to the chair. Then he attached electrodes to the wires and fastened them on points directly above Frank's eyes and on other parts of his body.

When he had finished, Karl stood with a control switch in his hand, waiting for his next order.

"I assure you, you are in the best of hands," the little man said. "Karl has never let anyone die of the pain—at least, not yet. But first I will give you one last chance. Will you tell all you know now—or will you find out how much agony you can take?"

"You're bluffing," replied Frank, praying that the man was.

"You have made your choice," said the little man. He raised his hand. "When my hand drops, the lesson begins."

He waited for one more endless second. Then his hand fell.

"No! STOP! I'LL talk!" Frank screamed, before Karl had a chance to throw the switch.

Startled, Joe stared at his brother. He hadn't expected Frank to give in so quickly, though he guessed he couldn't blame him. Joe thought that he himself might have held out longer, but you never could be sure of something like that.

The little man didn't seem surprised at all.

"I am glad to see that you are a sensible young man," he said.

Karl didn't seem surprised, either. "You Americans are all soft," he said with a thick German accent.

"Start talking," the little man ordered Frank. "Tell everything you know. As soon as you start holding back, or try to lie, we apply the shock."

"Don't worry, I'll tell you everything, everything," said Frank, with terror in his voice. "Why shouldn't I? As soon as I start squealing, I'm finished as far as the organization I work for is concerned, anyway. I might as well go all the way."

"You sound more and more intelligent with every word," the little man said. He was practically licking his chops.

"First, let me out of this chair," said Frank.

"Ah, but it is such a nice chair in which to sit and chat," said the little man. Karl nodded his agreement.

"Look, I have to get out of this thing, or else I'm going to be sick." Frank's voice was desperate.

"That would be rather unpleasant," the little man said. "Very well. We will let you out of the chair. But if you don't start talking right away, back in it you go—and no release then."

"Don't worry. I'll tell you everything."

"Karl, let our friend up," said the little man.

Karl looked cheated, but he obeyed. "Such a pity. I usually enjoy working on Americans," he said as he released the last steel band that fastened Frank to the chair.

"Not on this American," cried Frank, as he sent his fist out in a driving blow that caught Karl just above his heavy gut.

The big man doubled over with a loud "Oooof!" Frank leaned out of the chair and delivered a quick chop to the back of the neck.

Frank's karate teacher would have given a deep bow to the blow. Karl dropped to the floor as if felled by an ax.

Joe didn't waste time admiring his brother's skill. He quickly used his own skills, smashing into the little man with a football block that sent the cop sprawling. As soon as the man was on the ground, Joe's foot landed against his chin in a powerful kick.

Meanwhile, Denise had stopped looking weak and scared with a speed that made it clear it had all been an act. As the cop beside her pulled out his gun to go after Frank and Joe, she grabbed his gun arm and twisted it behind him. A moment later the snub-nosed revolver was in her hand with the barrel pressed against the side of the cop's head.

It all took less than a minute.

"Hey, neat work," Joe said to Frank. "You had me fooled for a second. I thought for sure you were caving in."

"I had to make it convincing. I had to wait as long as I could before I did my folding act," said Frank. "Of course, the closer I got to getting the shock, the easier it was to act scared."

"It did the trick, anyway," said Joe. "Now get these cuffs off me, and we'll get out of here."

Frank removed a ring of keys from the pocket of the unconscious little man. He had to try several of them before he found a key that snapped open Joe's handcuffs.

"Bring the cuffs over here," ordered Denise, who had forced her former guard to lie face-down on the floor. Expertly she handcuffed his hands behind him, then used his belt to tie his ankles together.

"We don't have to bother gagging him," she said. "As that little cop so thoughtfully informed us, this room is soundproof. It will take them quite a while to attract attention."

"Yeah, especially since Karl and the little guy are both out like lights. They look like they'll stay that way for a long time," added Joe. "Hey, Frank, you really connected with that monster."

"I put everything I had into the chop," said Frank. "I think it would have smashed a brick a foot thick. Maybe I should check to see how the guy is."

"No time for that," said Denise. "We have to worry about ourselves. Let's get out of here."

She led them from the room, and Frank used one of the keys on the ring to lock the door after they left. Then he and Joe followed Denise down a corridor to another steel door. Denise swung open the door, and they entered.

Frank and Joe froze. Waiting for them was a woman in a police uniform, complete with a pistol butt sticking prominently out of its holster.

But Denise didn't even raise the gun in her hand. "Boys, meet Marcelle," she said. "She's a friend—she works for the same organization I do."

Frank and Joe exchanged quick looks. The Gray Man's suspicions had been right. Reynard and Company did have agents within the Sûreté itself.

"She managed to inform me in my cell that she would be on duty this shift," said Denise. "Now if you two will turn your eyes away for a moment, Marcelle and I will do a quick striptease."

Frank and Joe turned around obediently and waited until they heard Denise say, "You can look now."

Denise modeled the police uniform she was wearing. "Not a bad fit," she said. "And the style is really quite good. The government got a famous designer to create it when they started admitting a large number of women into the force."

"Unfortunately, they'll take the loss out of my salary," said Marcelle as Denise tied her up securely. "They are not very understanding about things like this."

"Don't worry, your bonus from the boss will more than make up for it," said Denise. "And for this discomfort as well," she added, gagging Marcelle with a kerchief.

Denise took out her pistol and pointed it at the boys. "Come on," she said. "I am marching you two crooks out of here."

"What if someone tries to stop us?" asked Frank.

"This pistol is fully loaded, and I know how to

use it," Denise replied. "But let's hope it doesn't come to that. Shooting a policeman isn't very smart. It's the one thing that the law will never forgive under any circumstances."

The Hardys held their breath as they came to the front desk, but the guards were in the middle of an intense card game. They did little more than glance up as Denise, her gun drawn, herded Frank and Joe out onto the street.

"And these police are supposed to be the best in France," said Denise scornfully as they stood under the glow of a streetlight. Night had come and a misty summer rain was falling. "Now you see why it is so easy to work outside the law."

"Where do we go from here?" asked Frank.

"And how do we get there?" asked Joe. "We can't exactly hail a taxi."

"*You* can't even use the Metro," said Denise. "You can't afford it. Or have you forgotten?"

"That's right!" exclaimed Frank, clapping a hand to his forehead. "Our money! The wallets! The cops have everything!"

"A hundred and fifty thousand bucks," groaned Joe.

"I'm glad you are beginning to understand the situation you are in," said Denise. "You are now without money, and I suspect that you'll owe a very big explanation to whoever is financing you."

"Look, you've got to help us," said Frank.

"Can you take us into that building again—maybe we can get the money back," said Joe.

"And maybe I am crazy, but I don't think so," replied Denise.

"I've heard people say the French are heartless," commented Frank.

"Not heartless—merely practical," said Denise. "But maybe we can find a practical way to get you out of this tight spot."

"Get us out of it, and we'll do anything you want in return," promised Frank.

"The first thing I'll do is get you out of this neighborhood," said Denise. She walked to a small red car parked a few hundred feet away. "It's Marcelle's. She told me where it was and gave me the key."

Denise slid into the driver's seat and motioned for Frank and Joe to get in the back. They drove in silence for a half hour while the Hardys looked out the mist-beaded windows at the blurred black shapes of buildings and the streaky lights of neon signs as they traveled through Paris. Finally, Denise parked the car and got out. Frank and Joe followed her as she began walking briskly.

"My apartment is twenty blocks away," she said. "I didn't want to park too close. The police will search the immediate area where the car is found."

They walked the twenty blocks in fifteen minutes. Frank and Joe noticed that the buildings they passed were more and more elegant. The building that Denise lived in was truly luxurious, a mixture of nineteenth-century charm and modern convenience, such as the wrought-iron elevator, which rose swiftly and smoothly to the floor where Denise lived.

Her apartment was big and beautifully furnished, with floor-to-ceiling windows in the living room. Frank and Joe looked out one of them to see a broad avenue, and past that, trees illuminated by streetlights.

"That's the Bois de Boulogne, the finest park in Paris," Denise told them.

"This place must cost a fortune!" exclaimed Frank. "Reynard must give you an awful lot of dough."

"Yeah, it must be a great outfit to work for," Joe chimed in.

"Perhaps—if you can take the risks," Denise said coolly. "Wait here. I have to make a phone call—a private one."

She went into another room, closing a thick door solidly behind her.

Joe looked around the living room, at the Persian carpet on the floor, the modern paintings on the wall, the gleaming grand piano. It looked like something out of "Dynasty."

"I wonder who ever said crime doesn't pay?" he said.

"It does—until *you* pay for *it*," replied Frank.

"From the looks of things, Reynard has a lot of paying to do," commented Joe.

"Right," said Frank. "It's easy to see why the Network wants to get to the heart of its operation. Reynard and Company has to be doing an incredible amount of dirty work to make as much dough as it spreads around."

"This can only be one kind of money," said Joe. "Blood money."

They stopped talking when they heard the door opening. Denise returned to the living room.

"I have good news—and bad," she said.

"Give us the good news first," said Frank. "We need some right now."

"I have talked to my employers, and they have agreed to help you."

"What an honor," said Frank. "And to what do we owe this expression of trust? Have they run a background check on us and decided we're okay?"

"That wasn't necessary," replied Denise. "You see, there is no longer any danger of your going to the police under any circumstances—unless you want to commit suicide."

"What do you mean?" said Frank. "Obviously you know something we don't."

"Marcelle called the office a few minutes ago. You weren't kidding when you said you hit Karl hard. You hit him a little *too* hard."

"You mean—?" said Frank, already knowing

the answer from the grim look in Denise's eyes.

"That's right," Denise replied. "He's dead."

"That makes me a murderer!" Frank felt as if someone had smashed him in the solar plexus.

"And it makes your brother your accomplice," Denise went on. "But it's even worse than that."

"Yeah," said Joe, looking as bleak as his brother. "We're not just murderers. We're cop killers."

"Which means we're finished," said Frank. "No one can save us. No one."

Chapter

8

"YOU TWO ARE in luck," Pierre Reynard told Joe and Frank as they stood before Pierre, Maurice, and Yves. "We can save you."

Denise had taken the Hardys to the Reynards' private office and left them there.

"What does your company do—work miracles?" asked Frank.

"You don't need miracles," said Pierre. "All you need are a few changes in your appearance, another set of passports, a way to smuggle yourselves out of France, and tickets to Australia, Peru, or anyplace else where the French police or your former associates will not easily track you down."

"And you'll give us those things?" said Frank skeptically.

"We'll even give you enough money to resume

69

your business careers—perhaps by buying weapons to sell. We'll leave that to you. I'm sure you know how to make money. The size of the bankroll you so unfortunately lost is proof of that," said Pierre.

"That's real generous of you," said Frank.

"Reynard and Company is always happy to be of service to its clients, or rather, its former clients," Pierre told him.

"Look, let's stop beating around the bush," said Joe. "Tell us what you guys want us to do, and we'll tell you if we want to do it."

"*You'll* tell *us!* Don't make me laugh," cried Yves Reynard, but the smile on his face had nothing to do with laughter. It was the smile of a crocodile about to enjoy a meal.

"You have no money. You have no friends. And every cop in France would like to capture you—dead, not alive," said Maurice. "So you do what we say, or else we throw you out on the street, where you wouldn't last five minutes."

"Pardon my brothers' bluntness, but they are right, you know," added Pierre. "Unless, of course, you know someone else who will help you."

"You know we don't," said Frank.

The Hardys were on their own, on the wrong side of the law, caught in a trap they had to break out of themselves.

"Okay, okay, tell us about the job we have to do for you," said Joe.

"The job isn't for us," said Pierre. "It is for some clients of ours."

"Clients?" repeated Joe suspiciously. "Hey, what are you trying to pull?"

"We are not trying to 'pull' anything," replied Pierre patiently. "Since we are going to be working together, I suggest that you trust us. In business such trust is essential."

"Then why not start by trusting us and telling us just what your business is," countered Frank.

"Yeah," said Joe. "Gun running? Revolution? Terrorism? What?"

"All of them. And more. Yet at the same time, less. None of them, in fact," said Pierre.

"What are you talking about?" asked Frank.

"Cut the double talk," said Joe. "You might think it's funny, but we don't."

"You might say our business is 'funny business,' as you Americans put it," said Pierre. "You see, we at Reynard and Company don't plan or carry out crimes ourselves. We merely supply equipment and personnel to people who do.

"If you need a bomb and someone to set it off, you come to us. If you need a car and a driver to get away from a robbery, you come to us. If you need someone to tap a phone or steal a secret or forge a passport or provide any device or skill for which you might not want to put an ad in the newspaper, you come to us. We supply what you need."

71

Pierre smiled. "You see, a long time ago my brothers and I decided that there are people in every walk of life, whether they are doctors or lawyers, plumbers or politicians, who will sell or do anything for money. When our uncle left control of the firm to us, we made it our business to search out those people and hire them—to be used when needed. Our success speaks for itself. I am not boasting when I say that Reynard and Company is the greatest shopping center in the entire world of crime today."

"And you want to add us to your stock," said Frank.

"What if nobody wants us?" asked Joe. "Do you put us on sale for half price?"

"As I told you before—you're in luck," said Pierre. "There *is* someone who wants you, and for a handsome price."

"We *still* need to know what we have to do," said Frank. "Because there are some things we draw the line at."

"Then I suggest you get out your erasers before it is you who are rubbed out," replied Pierre.

He pressed a buzzer and spoke over the intercom. "Send Mr. Goya in."

He turned to the Hardys. "Try to look as tough as you can. Our client is coming to inspect the goods."

"Who is this guy?" Joe asked.

"Mr. Goya is a Basque nationalist; his people want to set up their own country in the Pyrenees

Mountains." Pierre smiled. "Needless to say, Spain and France object."

The door opened and Mr. Goya stepped into the room. He stroked his black beard, looking the boys over intently. "These two will do very nicely," he said.

Mr. Goya spoke in English, since no one else in the room spoke Basque, and he knew no French and refused to speak Spanish. The Spanish Civil Guard had executed too many of his comrades.

"Of course, we will have to make certain changes in their appearance," Pierre Reynard told Mr. Goya. "I would be less than an honest businessman if I did not inform you of that."

"I do not want any changes," replied Mr. Goya. "These two are perfect for this job the way they are."

"I assure you, the changes will be small and will in no way decrease the effectiveness of these two young men," said Pierre soothingly. He sounded like a garage mechanic assuring a customer that a car would need only minor repairs. "You see, the police have an eye out for them, so it will be necessary to alter the color of their hair and give them T-shirts with the name of a different rock group. Once that is done, there is no way for the police to pick them out of the swarm of punk rockers in the city, all with dyed hair and black clothing."

"I will have to see the results before I make a down payment," said Mr. Goya.

"That is fine with us," said Pierre. "Reynard and Company wants its clients to be completely satisfied."

Pierre pressed the intercom button again. "Send in Denise."

"Denise is our expert on the younger generation," he explained to Mr. Goya when Denise appeared.

After Pierre explained what was needed, Denise looked at the boys critically and said, "I think bright orange hair would be good for Frank, and a nice shade of purple for Joe. We'll get them a couple of T-shirts spray-painted with the words *Death Wish*. They're a hot new group that pretends to commit suicide on stage."

"How long will it take?" asked Mr. Goya.

"Not more than an hour," said Denise. "We have an excellent punk hairstylist on our payroll."

"And it will all be included in the original price," said Pierre. "We are not like *some* firms that give a low estimate and then pad the bill with extras."

"We will see," said Mr. Goya.

"Get moving," Pierre told Denise. "We don't want to keep Mr. Goya waiting any longer than necessary. He has important work to do."

"*Very* important," Mr. Goya agreed.

The young man to whom Denise took Frank and Joe said the job would be quite quick and easy. "The dye job these two have is the kind that

74

washes right out," he said, frowning. He gave his own spiked hair an approving pat. "I'll give them a real one—something that will last."

"Great," said Frank. "Just what we need."

"Yeah, thanks a million," added Joe. "I have to admit, though, I have some doubts. *Purple*. I mean, I always figured green was my color."

An hour later, when Denise returned the Hardys to the Reynards, Mr. Goya nodded once again. "They are even better than before. I will take them." Then he looked at Denise. "And what about the girl? Is she available? I can use her, too."

"Of course she is available," said Pierre. "Naturally, there will be a one-third additional charge."

"One-fifth," countered Mr. Goya.

"Let us not engage in vulgar haggling," said Pierre. "Let us say one-fourth."

"Done," said Mr. Goya. He pulled out his wallet and counted out a thick stack of large bills onto the desktop.

Pierre picked them up and counted them again while Yves and Maurice counted along with him. When they were done, they nodded.

"I'll take these people now, since I'm paying by the day," said Mr. Goya. "The faster they do the job, the better."

"Let's see, your checkout time is three A.M.," said Pierre, looking at his watch, and making a notation on a printed form that he handed to Mr.

Goya to sign. "We find this avoids disputes when the final payment is made."

"Did you explain the job to them?" asked Mr. Goya.

"We'll leave that to you," said Pierre. "I assure you, they will do anything you ask. And Reynard and Company backs up its service with an ironclad guarantee."

"We stand behind all our people," said Yves, giving Frank and Joe a meaningful look, and laying a revolver on the desk.

"We expect them to be very sharp," added Maurice, as he laid a wicked-looking switchblade beside the gun.

"I'm sure everyone gets your *point*," said Denise, giving Frank and Joe a piercing look of her own. "I'm sure nobody will forget it."

"Very well. Let's begin our work," said Mr. Goya. He led the Hardys and Denise out of the office. They rode the elevator down in silence. Not until they were seated in a dingy all-night café on a tiny deserted side street was Frank able to ask, "Okay, what are we supposed to do?"

"Yeah, give us the picture," said Joe. "What's the job?"

"*This* is the picture and your job," Goya said in a low voice. He removed a photo from his jacket pocket.

The Hardys and Denise leaned forward to look at it. They saw a young man wearing a black T-shirt, tight black trousers, and black combat boots, his spiky hair dyed lavender.

"His name is Carlos Gonzales," said Mr. Goya. "His father is one of the richest men in Spain and one of the greatest enemies of the Basque people. As you see in the picture, power-ful as the father is, he has not been able to stop Carlos from rebelling. Still, he must protect his son from kidnappers. Two detectives dressed like Carlos guard him constantly.

"Your job will be to separate Carlos from his guards and deliver him to me and a few friends of mine. How you do it is your job, but I'm sure a pretty girl and two such sympathetic-looking young men will have no trouble winning Carlos's confidence. And I am sure you can do it without a hitch. Our group has dealt with Reynard and Company before and has always been entirely satisfied."

"And you will be this time, too," Denise as-sured him.

"Just one thing," said Frank. "What will you do with Carlos? Hold him for ransom?"

"A very, very big ransom, which his loving father will be happy to pay for the return of his only child," replied Mr. Goya happily. Then he smiled, as if enjoying a private joke. "And of course we will return Carlos to this man we hate so very much. We will not deprive the father of his right to bury his son."

"You're going to—to kill him?" Frank's voice rose, then grew hushed.

"Even if the ransom is paid?" said Joe.

"Does that bother you?" asked Mr. Goya, giving the Hardys a searching look.

"Bother *these* two?" cried Denise. "What a foolish idea, Mr. Goya!" She leaned forward confidentially. "Frank and Joe have killed before. What difference will one more corpse make?"

Frank and Joe silently exchanged looks. How much deeper into crime would they get? As deep as murder?

Chapter

9

THE SUN WAS rising over Paris as Frank and Joe trudged back to their hotel. Mr. Goya had kept them up all night, planning the kidnapping of Carlos Gonzales.

Above them, the sky turned pink, then a pale and deepening blue. It gave the old buildings of Paris the glow of new life. But the Hardys saw none of it as they reached the chipped stone steps of their hotel.

"We can't refuse to go through with this," said Frank. "The Reynards will kill us in a minute. We know too much about their operation now for them simply to let us go."

Joe nodded. "And we can't go to the police. Cops don't cut deals with cop killers."

"Right," agreed Frank. "And we sure can't

turn to the Network for help." He sighed. "We're criminals on the run—the Reynards are offering us our only chance of escape."

"I wish we were back in Bayport right now," Joe said wistfully. "Dad thinks we're having a great time in New York."

"Instead, we're kidnapping a kid in Paris." Frank's fists clenched. "We have to stop that murder," he said, "even if it kills us."

By the time the Hardys met Denise late that night to carry out the kidnapping, they had a plan of their own.

Denise smiled as Frank and Joe sat down at the table in the café where she was waiting.

"How do I look?" she said, tossing her red hair back.

She wore a black blouse, a short black skirt, black fishnet stockings, and pointed black boots with silver buckles.

"It's not authentic punk style," she said, "but I don't think Carlos will mind. He's supposed to like pretty girls."

"Then he's sure to like you," said Joe. Looking at her, he had a hard time believing that someone so attractive could do such ugly things. He had to remind himself it was the Reynards' business to find people with special talents who would do anything for money. Denise definitely had the special talent for catching a man's eye.

"It's almost midnight," said Joe, looking at his

watch. "The action must be heating up. Time for us to get moving."

Their destination was Hollywood Heaven, the hottest disco in Paris. At the entrance, a doorman with a mohawk, wearing a leather motorcycle jacket, tight blue jeans, and a spike-studded belt shook his head as they approached.

His head stopped moving when Denise held a five-hundred-franc note in front of his eyes.

"*Entrez,*" he said, plucking the bill from her hand and swinging the door open in one swift motion.

"Money makes life so simple," said Denise as they entered the strobe-lit, barnlike room.

"And so dangerous—for Carlos Gonzales, anyway," added Frank, his eyes roaming the crowd, searching for the young man they had seen in the photo.

"There he is," said Joe, pointing quickly.

Carlos Gonzales was leaning against the bar, drumming his fingers to the deafening disco beat.

"Good eyes," said Frank.

"He was hard to miss with that pair of gorillas shadowing him."

Close to Carlos were two large men in red-colored wigs and black clothes that didn't quite fit. They were swaying to the music as if trying to keep their balance on a trembling tightrope. If they were trying to blend into the background, they weren't doing very well.

"Now comes the job of separating the boy

from the men," said Denise. She went about her job very well.

Within five minutes she was dancing with Carlos. Five minutes after that, he had forgotten about the music, waved away his guards, and was leading her to a table for a glass of champagne. Fifteen minutes later, Denise led him over to Frank and Joe, who were standing by a wall, looking bored and indifferent.

"Sam and Pete, meet Carlos," said Denise.

"Happy to meet you," said Carlos, smiling.

Frank and Joe kept their faces blank, ignoring the hand that Carlos extended.

"Hey, look, Carlos is okay," Denise said. "I vouch for him."

"Sure, I'm okay," Carlos spoke up.

"So, you're okay," said Frank coldly. "So what do you want?"

"Well, I hear from this lady that you guys know of a good party we could go to," Carlos said awkwardly. He might have learned to look tough, but the Hardys could see the uncertainty in his eyes.

"Yeah," Frank said, "but we're talking business here. If you two want to party, we'd be happy to help—but we like to be rewarded for our humanitarian efforts." He smiled wolfishly.

"I don't understand," Carlos said.

Joe poked a finger into Carlos's chest. "Let's see some *money*, wimp."

"Oh!" Carlos's face lit up. "No problem, *ami-*

gos. Money is something I understand." Carlos confidently pulled a well-stuffed wallet from his jeans.

"Are you *sure* this guy is okay?" Frank asked Denise warily.

"Don't worry about him," she answered.

"I don't know." Joe shook his head. "Something about him smells lousy." He jerked his head at the two bodyguards who still leaned against the bar, careful not to let the rich kid out of their sight. "I got a nose for stuff like that. Just who are those two goons?"

"Oh, *them*," Carlos said, looking embarrassed. "Don't worry about them. You see, I made a deal with my father. He promised not to interfere with anything I want to do, just so long as nobody tries to get at his money through me. So, I have guards."

"Guards mean law, and law means trouble," said Joe. "They'll bum out the party." Frank and Joe turned away.

"Come on, guys, give me a break," said Carlos.

"Okay, we'll party—but only if you shake those goons," said Joe.

Carlos looked torn. "But—"

"Okay. I'll find someone else to party with," said Denise. She turned away from Carlos, her body already beginning to move to the music.

"But how *can* we shake them?" asked Carlos desperately.

Denise turned back to him. "We only have to lose them for a few minutes—long enough to get away. As soon as we're outside, we'll make a break for it. Guys, meet us at the Café Duchamp, two blocks from here, in five minutes. Okay?"

"Okay," agreed Joe. "But don't be late—and you two better be alone."

"Trust me," said Denise.

"I hate to say it, but Denise is really good at this," said Frank as he and Joe watched her dance toward the exit with Carlos. The guards followed, pretending to dance, almost tripping over their own feet as they were jostled by the mob that packed the room tighter and tigher as the night wore on.

"Yeah, everything is going according to plan—*their* plan," said Joe as he and Frank elbowed their way through the dancers to stay close to the guards. "I hope *our* plan goes as well."

"That comes later," said Frank. "For the time being we have to follow orders."

Still dancing, Carlos and Denise disappeared out the door. The two guards froze in surprise. Then they charged through the crowd like full-backs, trying to reach the exit. Frank and Joe were right behind them. They ran out of the building in time to see the guards questioning the doorman, who shrugged his shoulders. However, when money was shoved into his hand, he promptly pointed in the direction that Carlos and Denise had gone.

The guards ran off at full speed. Frank and Joe waited a couple of seconds, then followed them, knees pumping, feet flying. They kept just enough distance so that the pounding of their combat boots on the pavement wouldn't alert the guards until they were out of sight of onlookers. Meanwhile, the disco doorman watched the two pairs of men dash off. He never even blinked his eyes. After a year at this job, nothing the customers did surprised him anymore.

Everything went according to plan. The guards weren't aware that they were being followed until Frank and Joe stepped up the pace to charge them. The guards stopped on the empty side street and wheeled around, automatically reached for their concealed shoulder holsters. But they were too late.

The Hardys already had guns in their hands—small but deadly Beretta pistols provided by Mr. Goya. The guards saw the weapons gleaming in the light of a streetlamp and, without being asked, raised their hands in the air.

The Hardys didn't have to say a word. They motioned with their pistols and their two prisoners turned around. The guards knew the rules of the game. The people who got their guns out first gave the orders.

Five minutes later the guards were gagged with heavy tape and tied hand and foot with unbreakable nylon cord, all supplied by Mr. Goya.

"Now," Frank said, "we have to put these two

away for a while. And *that* looks like a cozy spot." He pointed to a nearby trash dumpster.

"Yeah," said Joe. "Trash belongs with trash."

Prodding them with their pistols, they forced the two goons up and into the dirty green dumpster and shut the lid with a loud clang. Then they headed for the café.

"I can't believe this is going so smoothly," said Joe. "Like clockwork."

"That's the way Reynard's people are supposed to do things. They provide only the best service," replied Frank. "Let's hope we do as good a job when we start working on our own."

The Hardys reached the Café Duchamp. Carlos and Denise sat at a table, waiting for them. Carlos looked edgy, while Denise tried to take that edge off by giving him melting looks and touching his hand softly with hers.

Frank and Joe wore big grins as they strode toward the pair. "Ready to go?" Joe asked.

"Sure," said Carlos. "Do we take a taxi?"

"No need," said Frank. "We'll give you a lift."

They left the café, heading down a street lined with shops closed for the night toward a large, battered van.

"This is your van?" said Carlos. "Cool."

"And that's just how you'd better stay—cool," said Frank, pulling out his pistol.

"Please, do not hurt the girl," Carlos said, stepping in front of Denise.

"You poor jerk, you still don't get it," said Denise, stuffing a gag in his mouth from behind. "Now put your hands behind your back, Don Juan."

Bound and gagged, Carlos put up no resistance as the Hardys heaved him into the back of the van.

Denise locked the door and looked at her watch. "Our package is all tied up—and Goya won't be picking him up for forty minutes yet. Well, I guess the wait won't kill the kid."

"No, Goya will take care of that," said Frank.

"Right, murder wasn't part of our deal," agreed Denise. "That would have cost extra. But Goya will not have any trouble with *that*. He is very professional. He let us do the kidnapping. If we made a mistake, he would not be at risk."

"Let's be sure *we* don't run any risk now," said Joe. "Our job is over. Let's split."

"See you tomorrow morning at Reynard's," said Denise.

"They'd better pay off as promised, or—" Joe broke off, leaving his threat dangling in empty air.

"Or what?" asked Denise, smiling. "What could *you* do to the Reynards? But don't worry. They will pay. They are good businessmen, and they know how important it is to keep their end of a bargain."

"Yeah, good thing we're not dealing with crooks," said Joe as they left the van behind.

At the corner, Denise and the Hardys walked

off in opposite directions. Frank and Joe turned another corner, then stopped and waited.

"We'll give it five minutes before we head back to the van," Frank whispered.

"Too bad we can't call the cops and give them an anonymous tip to get to the van before Goya does," said Joe.

"We've already been over that," replied Frank. "The Reynards have spies on the force. They'd find out about the tip and suspect us immediately. We can't trust the police."

"But can we trust Carlos to play ball with us?" asked Joe.

"I think so," said Frank. "He'll be so grateful to be released that he'll do whatever we ask."

"Let's go over the story again to make sure it holds up," said Joe. "We tell Carlos we're undercover police, about to expose a gang of terrorists, right?"

"That's right," Frank answered. "And we're releasing him to save his life, but we don't want him to tell anybody that we did it, because that would blow our cover."

"So then he's supposed to issue a statement to the press saying it was Denise who let him go." Joe paused, looking unhappy. "Look, I can't do it. The Reynards will kill her."

"It would only be justice," Frank pointed out. "I have a hunch there's murder somewhere in her background."

"I don't think so," said Joe. "She's so young."

"And so pretty," Frank shot back. "That's what you really mean."

Joe nodded. "I just don't want her blood on my hands."

"I guess you're right," Frank said. "To tell the truth, I feel pretty queasy about it myself."

Joe grinned at his brother in gratitude. "I knew you couldn't do it either. You're not as cool and calculating as you try to act." Then Joe's face lit up. "Hey, how about this?" he cried. "Carlos can tell a story about working free of his bonds and smashing out of the van on his own. It will make him look like some kind of superhero."

Frank picked up on the idea. "We can do some smashing ourselves to make it look real. It might just work."

"Let's go." Joe led the way, his step springy, as if a giant weight had been lifted from his shoulders.

He and Frank sprinted around one corner and then the other. They looked down the street where the van was parked—still deserted.

"Carlos," Frank whispered, rapping on the door of the van.

"Boy," said Joe, "is he gonna be glad to see us."

The Hardys froze as the van door swung open.

Carlos wasn't glad. Carlos wasn't there at all.

Chapter

10

"How could Carlos have escaped?" Mr. Goya demanded.

"We don't know, but we will find out," Pierre Reynard said. His brothers nodded in menacing agreement.

Mr. Goya was meeting with the Reynards, Denise, and the Hardys in the Reynard offices. When the Hardys had discovered that Carlos was missing, they waited for Mr. Goya to arrive on the scene. As soon as they told him what happened, he phoned the Reynards on an emergency number, and the Reynards immediately ordered this predawn gathering.

Now Mr. Goya declared, "Certainly, you cannot expect me to pay for this mistake. I demand my down payment back."

"Of course we will return it," said Pierre. "We

are an honest business. Satisfaction guaranteed."

He removed an envelope from his desk drawer, gave it one last regretful look, and handed it to Mr. Goya.

Mr. Goya opened it, counted the bills inside, and said, "Fine." He rose from his chair. "I will be going now, and leaving this country. France no longer seems so comfortable to me."

"But I assure you, if you let us supply you with a different crew—" Pierre began to protest.

"No thank you," replied Mr. Goya. "In my business, I cannot afford people who make mistakes. Goodbye."

Putting the money in his pocket, he left the office.

Pierre waited until he was gone, then he said, "And in our business, we can't afford dissatisfied customers—or refunds."

While his brothers smiled grimly, Pierre picked up the phone, spoke a few quick words into it, then hung up.

"Mr. Goya will not be able to leave France," he said. "He will not even be able to leave this building. Not alive, anyway."

"Well, that's one way of handling complaints," said Frank, repressing a shudder.

Even Joe, who hated terrorists like poison, felt a chill run through him.

"Complaints are another thing we cannot afford," said Pierre. "Like Mr. Goya, we cannot afford people who do not do their jobs."

"I hope you are not referring to us," said Denise. "I assure you, we followed the plan perfectly."

"I am not referring to *you,* Denise," said Pierre. "You have proven yourself thoroughly capable in all your past assignments. But we do have two new employees about whom we know very little."

"Hey, you can't be talking about us!" exclaimed Frank. "We did everything we were supposed to do."

"We sure did," agreed Joe. "Denise will tell you that. Right, Denise?"

His look of appeal was met by Denise's cold gaze. "As far as I know," she said carefully.

Pierre glanced at his watch. "Let us find out whether the five A.M. news has anything to say about the affair."

He punched a button on his desk, and a TV set lit up on the wall. A woman newscaster was sitting next to a large photo of a young man. The young man was Carlos Gonzales.

Frank and Joe strained to figure out what the woman was saying, but she spoke too fast for them to understand.

They turned away from the screen to ask Denise—but the question never left their lips.

Denise was pointing a gun at them.

Frank and Joe wheeled around to face the Reynards. Guns were in their hands as well.

"According to the newscaster, Carlos reported

that he was set free by the two young men who abducted him in the first place," said Pierre. "Who they are and why they did it remains a mystery."

"But not to us," said Denise. "You two must have been fools enough to think you could trust a weakling like Carlos. And worse fools if you hoped to bargain for mercy from the police by setting him free. Obviously, you did not believe us when we told you what the police will do to cop killers. At least we can be sure you did not go to the police. If you had, you would be dead."

"Good thinking, Denise," said Pierre, nodding in approval.

"I try to earn my pay," replied Denise modestly.

Joe flashed Frank an apologetic look. *This* was the pretty girl he hadn't wanted to endanger?

Frank didn't notice Joe. He was too busy looking at the guns trained on them.

"Hey, you can't think—" he began.

"We don't *think* anything," snapped Pierre. "We *know*."

"We also know what to do about it," said Yves.

"The only question is how, when, and where," added Maurice. "And I say here, now, and with *this*." He raised the pistol in his hand.

"Not so fast," said Pierre, with cool executive authority. "Let us follow proper business procedures and avoid the difficulties that would be caused by going outside established channels. This is a job for our disposal department."

"But they're busy now," protested Maurice, looking at his pistol and then at the Hardys like a child deprived of a treat.

"Disposing of Mr. Goya should take them only an hour or so," said Pierre. "Then they can do the same with these two traitors."

"But what do we do with them in the meantime?" asked Yves.

"Why do you not store them in the corporate boardroom until they are taken?" suggested Denise. "No one ever goes in there—it is used only a few times a year. And it has a good lock on the door."

"I can see that you are trying to earn a raise, and you well may get it," said Pierre, smiling with approval.

"The cost of living is going up." Denise shrugged her shoulders and smiled sweetly in return. Then she motioned with her pistol, herding the Hardys out of the Reynards' private office.

The boardroom was furnished with a long, heavy oak table and high-backed oak chairs. Its walls were paneled with oak and its massive door was oak, too. It looked strangely old-fashioned in the otherwise sleek and modern headquarters of Reynard and Company.

"Our beloved uncle feels at home here when he

comes twice a year to preside over our public meetings," Pierre explained in answer to the Hardys' unspoken question as they looked around. "We go to great trouble not to interfere with the dream world of the respectable past that he lives in, as you can see from those pictures." He indicated the large framed portraits and photo enlargements that lined the walls. "You can amuse yourself by studying Uncle Paul's life while you wait for your death."

"You won't get away with this," Frank warned.

"Won't we? You doubt the efficiency of Reynard and Company? Then complain to our dear uncle, or at least to his pictures up there." Pierre and the others backed out of the room, and the heavy oak door swung shut behind them.

There was the sound of a lock being turned, and then silence.

"Who could have done it?" muttered Frank, his brows furrowed. "Who could have sprung Carlos and then framed us? I need time to figure it all out."

"Look, Sherlock, we don't have time for that. We have to figure out how to escape from here—and fast."

The Hardys thought for a moment.

Frank spoke for both of them when he said, "As far as I can see, there's nothing we can do but wait."

"Yeah," agreed Joe bitterly. "And like Pierre said, we can amuse ourselves looking at those pictures."

"I guess it's better than nothing." Frank started walking around the windowless room, looking at one picture after another.

"You can see how much the Reynards want to butter up their uncle Paul," Frank said.

"Yeah, just look at him," Joe whispered in awe.

There were full-length paintings of Paul Reynard over the years. Paul Reynard as a boy in short pants on a pony. Paul Reynard as a teenager in a school uniform. Paul Reynard as a young army officer. Paul Reynard as a white-haired gentleman in a tuxedo. There were enlarged newspaper photos of Paul Reynard receiving a medal from a high government official and another of Paul Reynard presiding over a meeting of the board of directors of Reynard and Company with his nephews looking on humbly in the background.

"I can see why he likes to live in the past," said Frank. "He has quite a distinguished past to live in."

"He looks like he's still having a good time," said Joe. "Look at this picture."

The picture was a blown-up page from the sports section of a British newspaper. It was dated a few months earlier. On it was a photo of Paul Reynard in formal clothes standing beside a large gray horse with a garland of flowers around its neck and a grinning jockey on its back. The headline at the top of the page read, "French Horse Wins Grand National Steeplechase."

Frank leaned forward to read the accompanying story.

"Hey, this is interesting," he said. "It's all about how Paul Reynard has devoted himself to breeding Percheron horses to become steeplechase racers. It seems that centuries ago Percherons used to carry Norman knights into battle, but after that they were used only as farm horses, and in recent years the breed has been dying out. Paul Reynard has turned his family estate in Normandy into a horse-breeding ranch and has now 'restored the Percherons to their former glory.' "

"His nephews must love that," said Joe. "It's kept their uncle busy and out of their hair."

Frank was still reading the article. "It says his estate is located close to the town of Bayeux, near the English Channel. The paper calls his arrival on the English racing scene 'the most devastating invasion since William the Conqueror sailed from that same Norman coast to take over England almost a thousand years ago.' "

"Remind me to write him a fan letter if we ever get out of this alive," said Joe, with a grimace of impatience at his brother. Leave it to Frank to get involved in picking up some weird information when there were so many more pressing things to do—like coming up with a plan for the moment the conference room door swung open.

"We might be able to do more than write him a letter," said Frank, his eyes lighting up.

"What do you mean?" asked Joe, who recognized the look on his brother's face. It was the look that appeared when Frank came up with the solution to an especially difficult problem.

"This picture has given me an idea," Frank replied. "Two ideas, actually."

"What are they?" Joe asked eagerly.

But before Frank could answer, they both heard a sound that cut their conversation off.

It was a key being inserted in the lock.

"Too late," groaned Joe, his brief flare of hope dying.

Their executioners had arrived.

Chapter

11

THERE WAS NO time for Frank to explain his idea, just a few desperate seconds to try it out.

He grabbed one of the paintings on the wall, and ran to one side of the doorway. Immediately Joe grabbed another, and ran to the other side. When Frank raised the picture high above his head, Joe got the idea. He grinned, then tensed, pressing against the wall as the door swung open.

Two men entered the room, moving with confidence that came from the guns in their hands. Both were already inside before they hesitated and started to look around for their victims.

That was all the time Frank and Joe needed. The paintings came crashing down on the men with massive force. The canvases ripped on impact, and the heavy frames were forced over the men's heads and shoulders, pinning their arms to their sides. They kicked and struggled, but it did no good.

Seconds later, the men collapsed like puppets with their strings cut. They were feeling no pain. The Hardys' fists had done a good job of knocking them out.

Frank looked down at them. "Well, we're not the only ones who've been framed now."

Joe laughed. "And the Reynards aren't the only ones with guns on their side." Joe stooped to grab one man's weapon, while Frank took the other. "Let's go get them," cried Joe.

Frank shook his head. "And what do we do if we manage to capture them?"

"We turn them over to the cops and—" Joe stopped. Then he said, "I see what you mean."

"Right. We can't show ourselves to the police. Not only would they not believe our story, they'd arrest us as cop killers, and our chances of beating the rap would be zilch since we can't get the Network involved."

"So what do we do? Where do we go?" asked Joe, looking with disgust at the now-useless gun in his hand.

Frank stuck his gun in his pocket. "What we do is go to the only man who can turn the Reynards over to the police and end the criminal activities of Reynard and Company forever. The man who owns it. Paul Reynard himself."

Frank nodded toward the blowup of the newspaper story about Paul Reynard's success as a horse breeder. "It says here that the name of his place in Normandy is—surprise, surprise—Chateau Reynard. Between Bayeux and the coast. Come on. Let's get out of here fast, before the regular employees start coming to work."

"First, though, we need money," said Joe, stooping over to relieve one of the men of his wallet. "We'll need tickets, among other things."

"These guys are pretty well-heeled for hoods," said Frank, taking the other wallet and looking at the bills stuffed inside.

"Probably got paid in advance for killing us," said Joe.

Cautiously the Hardys stepped into the corridor. It was empty.

"Are they gone?" Joe asked.

"I'll bet the Reynards and Denise have gone home to sleep," whispered Frank.

"Yeah, they had a hard night's work," said Joe as they crept toward the exit. "Funny, we've been up all night, and I don't even feel tired."

"There's nothing like the danger of death to keep you alert," replied Frank as they reached the deserted reception area. He checked the front door. "We're in luck. We can unlock it from the inside just by turning this knob."

It wasn't until they reached the Gare St. Lazare—the cavernous old railway station for trains to Normandy, one of many that dotted the

French capital—and were aboard the early-morning train for Bayeux, that Joe was able to say, "I guess a little shut-eye wouldn't hurt now."

He leaned back in the upholstered seat and dozed off, watching the scenery gradually change from urban to suburban and finally rural. Joe felt as if he'd been asleep for not more than five minutes when he was shaken awake.

"Just a few more minutes," he groaned. "I don't have any classes until—" Then he remembered where he was. "We're here already?"

"Yup," said Frank. "Now to find out where we go from here. We need a map."

They found a detailed one in a shop catering to tourists near the medieval cathedral that dominated the town. The map showed the sites of notable buildings in the area. Chateau Reynard was one of them.

"It's marked in red," said Frank. "Let's see what that means." He studied the map for a moment longer and said, "It means 'not open to visitors.' "

Frank and Joe went to the chateau, anyway. They rented bicycles, since there was no chance of two wild-looking punks renting a car without ID. Even the bike shop let them pedal away only after they left a deposit equal to the full value of the bikes.

Under a broiling sun, sweat soaking their clothes, they biked for almost an hour through gently rolling hills shaded by flowering apple trees and bright green pastures dotted with cows and horses. They traveled the final two miles on a deserted, winding one-lane asphalt road that turned off just past a crudely lettered wooden signpost reading, Ch. Reynard.

"Not open to visitors is putting it mildly," said Joe, staring at the stone wall surrounding the estate. It was over ten feet high, and on its top, jagged shards of broken glass embedded in concrete glinted in the sunlight. "I guess this is what you call French hospitality."

"We'll have to figure out some way of getting over that wall," said Frank.

"Look, I know you like to make complicated plans and all, but why don't we try something simple for a change?" suggested Joe.

"Like what?"

"Like this." Joe walked up to the huge wooden door barring the entrance to the chateau grounds and pulled a rope that set a bell clanging.

After a couple of minutes, the door swung open a crack. The face of a very large man peered out.

"Do you speak English?" asked Joe.

"A leetle," the man said.

"We'd like to see Mr. Paul Reynard on very important business."

"No!" the man growled in the same kind of tone an attack dog might use.

The door slammed shut, and a moment later the Hardys heard the bolt slide into place.

"Well, so much for doing things the easy way,"

said Joe. "I wonder why the guy was so unfriendly."

"It wouldn't surprise me if the nephews bribed the old man's servants to keep strangers away from him," replied Frank, who was already studying the wall. "Not to mention our purple and orange hair."

"Makes sense," agreed Joe, and joined his brother at the wall. "See any way over?"

Frank stared upward a moment longer, then nodded. "I think so. It's worth trying, anyway. Come on."

He walked his bike along the wall away from the door, and Joe followed. The wall went on and on.

"This estate must be immense," said Frank.

"I guess the horses need lots of space to run. Hey, let me in on your plan—unless you'd rather go it alone."

"No. I'm going to need your help," said Frank, finally stopping. "We're far away from the entrance now, so there's a good chance no one will spot us when we go over the wall—which is a chance we'll have to take. I don't want to wait until dark. The nephews are probably hunting for us already. And that servant who saw us might put them on our trail."

"But how do we get over the wall?" asked Joe. "Did I ever tell you that you have a really lousy habit of keeping your plans secret? I think you do it just to make me mad."

"You're right," Frank said with a grin. "But I will tell you, this plan goes in several stages. First, there's *this*."

Frank leaned his bike against the wall and told Joe to steady it for him. Then he stood on its seat, emptied the contents of his jacket pockets, and tossed the jacket up, draping it over the top of the wall.

"That should take the edge off those pieces of glass—I hope," he said, climbing down from the bike.

He handed his pistol to Joe, saying, "Keep this for a few minutes. I'll take *this* with me."

He picked up the compact coil of thin but strong nylon rope left over from tying Carlos and his guards in Paris and jammed it in his pocket.

"Now stand over here, about three feet from the wall, and make a stirrup with your hands."

"I see," said Joe, the light dawning. He did as Frank instructed, standing near the wall and lacing the fingers of his hands together to form a stirrup. Meanwhile, Frank had backed off to have room to make his run.

"Now, remember, as soon as my feet hit your hands, give it your best heave—that wall is *high*."

"Don't worry. Although I don't see why you always get the fun part," said Joe.

"Because I thought of it first," replied Frank, and started his run.

When he was a few feet from Joe, Frank

leaped, his feet smacking into the palms of Joe's linked hands. At the moment of impact, Joe heaved upward with every ounce of his strength as Frank used Joe's hands as a springboard. Joe looked upward to see the bottoms of Frank's feet as they sailed up to the top of the wall.

"Pretty good," Joe had to admit. "A little stronger jump would have let you somersault right over, though."

Frank carefully lowered himself down the other side. A couple of minutes later, a rock with one end of the nylon cord tied onto it came flying from inside the compound, to land next to Joe.

He grabbed the cord, tested it to make sure it was firmly secured on the other end, and climbed hand over hand up the side of the wall. Once on top, he lowered himself down the other side until he hung suspended by his fingertips. Then he let go, dropping the rest of the way to the ground.

Frank was waiting for him. But he wasn't alone.

"Hi," Frank said. "As you can see, we're among friends here."

Three large pearl-gray horses had walked over to investigate the visitors, clearly hoping for sugar. They nuzzled the pockets of Joe's jacket.

"Sorry, pals," Joe told them. "Just a couple of pistols."

"Let's hope we don't need them," said Frank, as Joe handed him his gun. "Well, we're over the wall. Now we have to get into the chateau itself."

They looked at the chateau, separated from them by a wide pasture. It was a rectangular gray stone building, taller than it was wide. Some distance away were other, lower buildings, probably stables.

"It's a funny shape," said Joe.

"That's the Norman style of building. I remember seeing pictures of it in a book on architecture I read last year."

"Someday your head will burst open and a ton of trivia will come pouring out," said Joe. "Come on, let's get moving."

"Not so fast." Frank held up his hand in warning. "We'll have to take it slow. There's not much cover, and we don't want to be seen."

He crouched down in the high grass. Joe reluctantly did the same. Together, they started creeping toward the chateau, at times actually slithering on their stomachs to get across open areas.

"Sometimes I think you play it a little too safe," Joe said, panting as they wiggled into the cover of an apple tree.

"It's better to be safe than sorry." Frank looked over his shoulder at Joe as he led the way to a hedgerow near the chateau.

At that moment, he saw Joe's mouth drop open. Then his brother's whole body froze.

He whirled around to find out what Joe was looking at—and he froze, too.

He no longer saw the chateau growing larger as they came closer.

He saw two black holes less than a foot from his eyes.

He was staring into a double-barreled shotgun.

He opened his mouth to say something, but almost immediately he heard the sharp click of the firing hammer being cocked.

Chapter

12

"DON'T SHOOT—YET," said a voice from behind the gunman.

Frank and Joe looked up. The large man who had turned them away from the chateau was now training a shotgun on them. At his side appeared a man in elegantly cut riding clothes, complete with gleaming leather boots and a riding crop in his hand. The Hardys recognized him instantly. He was Paul Reynard.

"When Emile told me he had turned away two young American visitors, I reprimanded him for his inhospitality," said Paul Reynard. "I sent him back to let you in. But he found that you had left. Then, trying to follow you to give you my invitation, he came upon your bikes and guessed you went over the wall. Now I must ask you to explain yourselves, or else you will be turned over to the police."

"We'd like nothing better than to explain ourselves," said Frank, as he and his brother got to their feet, Emile's shotgun still trained on them.

"That's why we came over the wall—to talk to you," added Joe.

"You must have something very important to discuss since you went to such trouble," said Paul Reynard. "Come inside and we will talk. But I am afraid that Emile will have to keep his gun on you. We are a bit suspicious of intruders."

When they entered the chateau, the Hardys saw why Paul Reynard was wary of intruders. The outside of the building might have been forbidding gray stone, but the inside was filled with beautiful, costly paintings, furniture, and carpets.

Paul Reynard took great pride in his home. In fact, he paused to point out some of his more outstanding possessions: a three-hundred-fifty-year-old painting by Rubens and a much more modern one by Picasso, a table from the court of Louis XIV, a chair that Napoleon himself once sat on, and a carpet woven in Persia a century ago.

He was apparently willing to give them a guided tour of the whole chateau, but Frank said, "I don't mean to seem rude, but there is a lot we have to tell you, and we should do it as quickly as possible."

"Oh, don't worry about proving your innocence," Paul Reynard said. "I believe it already, just by your reactions to the pieces I pointed out to you. They were not the reactions of thieves, but of polite visitors. You see, I pride myself on being a good judge of character. It is a skill I perfected many years ago. I was an officer in French Army Intelligence in Algeria, and I had to learn to tell the difference between friends and enemies among the natives." He smiled. "Even though the natives never dressed like *les punks*."

"Thanks for your confidence in us," said Frank. "I just hope that what we tell you doesn't shake your confidence in yourself—as a judge of character."

"What do you mean?" asked Paul Reynard.

"I'm talking about your nephews," replied Frank.

"The ones who are running your business," added Joe.

"My nephews? Is there something wrong?"

"Maybe we should talk in private," said Frank, glancing at Emile, who was hovering near them just within earshot. Frank hoped they had not already said too much.

"Come into my study," said Reynard, his face changing. "I want to hear everything you have to say."

Forty minutes later, after Frank and Joe had explained in detail how the nephews had been making their profits, Paul Reynard shook his head in a mixture of dismay and anger.

"I suspected that something was going on in my company. Our profits have been good—*too* good to be the result of honest trading. But I never dreamed our profits were blood money." His voice grew steely. "Those scum. They are staining the Reynard name. I will show them what a mistake they make in thinking I am a helpless old man. I will make sure they go to prison for the rest of their lives."

He turned to the Hardys. "But what can I do to repay you for this information? I know you must be risking a great deal to tell it to me."

"Just forget you ever saw us," said Frank.

"And get us out of the country without anyone else seeing us," said Joe.

Paul Reynard nodded. "Say no more. My military-intelligence experience taught me the need for discretion in undercover activities. I will be happy to do what you ask."

Frank and Joe looked at each other and grinned. Just a short time earlier, their mission had seemed a total failure. Now it was turning into a complete success. It was almost too good to be true.

"Let us have champagne to toast my revenge," said Paul Reynard, pulling a bell cord. A moment later, Emile appeared, this time without his gun.

"Champagne," Paul Reynard commanded.

"I'm afraid we're not really into drinking," said Frank.

"Though a couple of Cokes would hit the spot," added Joe.

"Oh, you Americans," said Paul Reynard, and told Emile to bring two bottles of soda along with the champagne.

The Cokes arrived already poured over cracked ice in tall elegant glasses. The Hardys waited for Paul Reynard to open his champagne bottle and make a toast before they drank.

Paul Reynard expertly pulled the cork from the bottle—but the pop of the fizzing champagne was drowned out by a loud noise from outside.

"There's an army base nearby here," Paul Reynard explained. "Their training helicopters insist on flying low over the countryside. You can imagine the effect they have on my horses, but my complaints to the authorities have been useless."

Then he raised his glass and the Hardys raised theirs.

"To victory over crime," Paul Reynard said.

"To victory," Frank and Joe exclaimed together, their voices slightly hoarse, throats parched after their long, hot, hard day.

But the glasses didn't reach their lips.

"Such a nice party. We couldn't stand not being invited," said a familiar voice.

It belonged to Pierre Reynard, who was standing in the doorway, a pistol in his hand. He was not alone.

As he entered the room, he was followed by his two brothers, as silent and sinister as ever.

Next came Denise, her pretty face grim.

Then two more people entered the room.

"What the—?" cried Frank.

"It can't be!" exclaimed Joe.

The last two people *couldn't* be real. They had to be ghosts, the ghosts of the gangster Jacques, who had died in the shoot-out with the police, and the ghost of Karl, the policeman whose death had made the Hardys murderers.

Chapter

13

"THE LOOK ON the faces of you two Americans! It alone was worth the trip down here," said Pierre, chuckling. They had gathered in the chateau's drawing room. The Hardy brothers and Paul Reynard were sitting together on a couch. The Reynard nephews sat on a couch facing them. Beside the Reynards, Denise sat on Napoleon's chair, while Jacques, Karl, and Emile stood with their guns drawn. "You looked like you were seeing ghosts," Pierre went on, still smiling.

"Do you blame us?" said Joe.

"I'll let Denise explain the whole thing to you."

"She doesn't have to," replied Frank. "I've figured it out."

"Oh, come now," said Pierre disbelievingly.

"You don't know my brother," said Joe. "He probably has figured it out."

"You staged that phony police capture of us as a test to see if we were reliable," said Frank. "You probably do it to all new customers you aren't sure of. And when I knocked out Karl, you saw your chance to blackmail us since you needed a couple of guys like us for the Carlos snatch."

"So it wasn't the police who captured us, it was a bunch of Reynard crooks in disguise," said Joe.

"Very good," said Pierre, nodding. *"Too* good, in fact, for a pair of punk criminals. But your coming to my dear uncle here already told me that. It was quite a surprise when Emile called us to say a couple of young Americans had come knocking on the door. It was a good thing we had a high-speed helicopter to get us here. Now you can spare yourselves a lot of unpleasantness by telling us who you really work for."

"That's right," said Denise. "For your sakes, I suggest you tell us immediately."

"Why should we?" asked Frank. "Whether we do or don't, you're not going to let us leave this place alive."

"And I bet Karl doesn't have one of his 'truth machines' handy," said Joe.

"No, he doesn't," replied Pierre. He smiled. "He has something better. Do you want to tell the

Americans what Karl can use here, Uncle?"

"You swine," said Paul Reynard through clenched teeth. "You will never get away with this."

"And who will stop us, Uncle?" asked Pierre. "You, unfortunately, will soon die of a fall from one of your beloved horses. And of course these two Americans will never be heard from again."

Pierre turned back to Frank and Joe. "Since my uncle seems unwilling to reveal one of the most fascinating features of the chateau, I will do it for him. After all, it will soon belong to my brothers and me. So I will personally take you on a guided tour."

He nodded at Jacques and Karl, who in turn motioned with the guns for the Hardys to rise.

"You come, too, Denise," said Pierre. "In your new position, you should know as much as you can about our operations. That's why we've brought you along on this trip."

"I've been promoted," Denise told the Hardys.

"There has been public pressure to have a woman on our board of directors," explained Pierre. "Denise will fit the bill very nicely. Of course, she will have to change from her current style of dress to a more executive look."

"With the salary I'll be getting," said Denise, "I'll be able to buy my clothes from the best designers in Paris."

"Just be careful not to put any of that cash in

your pockets," said Frank bitterly. "Bloodstains don't wash out."

"That's the last time I'll ever go for a pretty face," muttered Joe.

"It's the last time you will ever do *anything*," Pierre corrected him. "But now let me show you something in this house that is far more interesting than paintings and furniture."

Pierre and Denise used their guns to herd the Hardys out of the room and down a corridor lined with mirrors in gilt frames.

"My family built this house a hundred and seventy years ago, after they had become successful businessmen. But long before that, the Reynards were barons who added to their estates by seizing those of their neighbors. The house was built on the ruins of our family castle . . ."

Frank and Joe found themselves staring down a stone stairway descending into musty-smelling darkness.

". . . Especially the family dungeons," said Pierre, who snapped a switch that lit the stairs. "Go. There is still more to see."

Lights had been installed in the damp, cold stone underground chambers where daylight never penetrated.

The Hardys were able to peer through the slots in thick iron doors to see narrow cells without a stick of furniture in them.

"The best is yet to come," Pierre announced as he opened the door to a much larger chamber.

"Enter and see one of the finest collections of its kind in the world."

In the chamber was a bewildering array of strange-looking instruments.

"This is a rack, on which a human being can be stretched until he is literally torn apart," said Pierre. "And this is a press, which gradually crushes a person to death. Here is my favorite—a cutting machine that will neatly slice off fingers, toes, and even whole arms and legs. Medieval tortures were quite ingenious, and my ancestors collected only the very best." He paused, and then smiled. "You will notice how excellently these instruments have been preserved. They are all in perfect working order."

"You can't intend to—" Frank began, but couldn't bring himself to finish the sentence.

"You've got to be crazy," said Joe.

"It is you who are crazy—if you do not talk," said Pierre. "You may die in any case, but I assure you that Karl can use these instruments to make you beg for death."

"He's right, you know," said Denise. "Be sensible."

"Why should we listen to you?" exclaimed Joe.

"Then listen to your own fears," said Pierre. "I think an hour in one of these cells will give you enough time to see reason. And if you don't, Karl is eager to have his fun."

Minutes later, the Hardys found themselves

locked in one of the cells, staring at the iron door. Suddenly the door vanished.

The light had been turned off. The cell was pitch black.

Joe heard only the sound of Frank's voice.

"There's no way out."

Chapter
14

"LISTEN," FRANK WHISPERED in the darkness of the dungeon cell.

Someone was turning the key in the door.

"We'll try to jump him when he comes in," Joe whispered back. "I'll stand on the right. You stand on the left. It's our last chance."

The door swung open. Electric light from the corridor poured into the cell to reveal Frank and Joe pressed to the wall on either side of the doorway.

But no one entered the cell.

"Forget about the surprise you were planning," Denise called from the corridor. "I am not stupid enough to fall for that. Back up, both of you."

The Hardys could be sure she had a gun in her hand. Shrugging, they retreated to the center of the cell. From there, they could see Denise framed in the open doorway.

Her hands were empty except for the door key. And she was alone.

The Hardys braced themselves to make a charge at her.

"Relax, idiots," she said, as if talking to small children. "Can you not see that I am here to help you escape?"

"You mean you've been sent to persuade us to tell the Reynards what they want to know, and save them the trouble of using their torture machines," said Joe.

Denise shook her head. "You are slow to understand. It is bad enough that I must reveal my identity in order to save your lives. The least you could do is cooperate. We do not have much time before the Reynards come down here after you."

"Your identity?" Frank repeated. "You mean—"

"That's right," replied Denise. "I work for the French Sûreté. I have been investigating the Reynard operation for two years now. I had just a few more pieces of the puzzle still to piece together to complete the picture when you two came along to complicate matters."

"So it was *you* who freed Carlos," cried Frank.

"Now you understand," said Denise.

"And you arranged for him to frame us for it so the Reynards wouldn't suspect you," Frank went on.

"You were willing to throw us to the wolves like pieces of meat," said Joe.

"I thought you were a couple of punks who deserved any punishment you got," said Denise. "That was before you escaped to see Reynard and expose his nephews. But what are you smiling at, Joe? A private joke?"

"Yeah, a private joke," said Joe, who was smiling ruefully.

"My brother is thinking that you're a lot tougher than you look, and a lot tougher than, say, we would have been in that spot," spoke up Frank.

Denise shrugged. "The Sûreté does not hire weaklings. But I still don't know who you work for."

"No soap," said Joe, shaking his head. "This may be another trick to get us to reveal ourselves."

Denise nodded. "I see that you are professionals, too," she said. "You can tell me about yourselves later—after we get out of here."

"*If* we get out of here," Frank corrected her, as he heard footsteps approaching.

"Quiet," whispered Denise, and turned to greet Karl and Jacques.

"What are you doing here?" asked Karl.

"I thought a little feminine persuasion might tempt them to talk," Denise replied, flashing Joe a quick look of gratitude for the idea.

"That won't be necessary," said Karl, with a

wolfish grin. "Pierre told me to take them to the torture room now and start softening them up."

Karl couldn't wait to start. He pulled his pistol from his pocket and snarled, "Come on, you two. It is truth time. Get mov—"

Then two things happened almost instantly.

Denise's hand came down on the wrist of Karl's gun hand in a karate chop that sent the gun dropping from fingers that had gone limp as spaghetti. A second later, both of her hands sent him flying through the air to smash against the wall.

Before Karl even hit the floor, Denise had wheeled to send her fist smashing against Jacques's jaw. His eyes glazed over, his knees buckled, then his body collapsed to the floor.

"What are you waiting for?" Denise asked the Hardys, who were watching the action open-mouthed. "Do something."

"You mean you actually need some help?" exclaimed Joe. Shaking off his awe at her efficiency, he jumped Karl, who was struggling to rise to his feet. The impact of Joe's body, and then of his fist, sent Karl back to the floor. He went out like a light.

"Shall we lock them in the cell?" asked Joe.

"I don't think so," answered Denise. "If they awaken soon, they might bang loudly enough on the door to attract attention."

"I've got an idea," said Frank. "We can give them a taste of their own medicine."

He grabbed Karl's arms and dragged his unconscious body out of the cell and toward the torture chamber. Joe got the idea and did the same with Jacques.

A few minutes later, both crooks were securely locked in place—Karl spread-eagled on the rack, Jacques with a crushing weight dangling over his body. Then they were gagged with their own shirts.

"When they come to, they'll have lots of time to think about what torture really feels like," said Frank as he, Joe, and Denise tiptoed down the corridor and to the stairway.

"Let's hope that by the time they're released, we're far away from here," said Joe.

"We should be," replied Denise. "They've left the helicopter unguarded."

"I hope I can handle it," said Joe. "I've had some flight training on American machines, but I've never used a French control board."

"Neither have I," said Frank.

"Don't worry about that," said Denise. "I have."

"I should have known," muttered Joe.

"Is there anything you *can't* do?" asked Frank.

"Cook," Denise answered with a grin.

They had reached the ground floor of the chateau and were moving cautiously down an empty corridor.

"Which exit do we use?" asked Joe.

"We cannot leave yet," said Denise. "We must make one more stop."

"What?" asked Frank. Then, before Denise could answer, he said, "Of course. Paul Reynard."

"Good thinking."

"Elementary," said Frank, unable to resist using the favorite word of his favorite detective. "Where did they lock him up?"

"In his study. Fortunately, they gave me the key."

"It's lucky they trust you," commented Joe.

"Luck has nothing to do with it," said Denise. "I spent two long hard years winning that trust. I don't like to think of some of the things I had to do."

They reached the study door, but before they entered, Frank glanced around. "Where are the nephews?" he whispered.

"Celebrating your capture with champagne," said Denise. "And looking forward to inheriting Reynard and Company, not to mention this property and the Reynard stables. When I left them, they were talking about using drugs on the horses to win big purses."

"Nice guys," said Joe. "Anything they wouldn't do for money?"

"If there is, I haven't discovered it." Denise unlocked the study door.

Paul Reynard was sitting at his desk. His ex-

126

pression turned icy when he saw Denise. Then he smiled when he saw the Hardys behind her.

"You've come to save me," he exclaimed. "I knew that a young lady so beautiful would not be capable of committing such ugly crimes."

"Good to know I'm not the only one who's a sucker for a pretty face," said Joe with a grin.

"Thank you for your gallantry, but we have no time for it," said Denise, all business. "We must get to that helicopter fast."

"Then I was right," said Paul Reynard. "You really are trying to save me. This is not just a ruse to win the confidence of these young men."

"Of course I am trying to save you," replied Denise. "The Sûreté frowns upon the murder of innocent people."

"I apologize. My experience in army intelligence taught me always to be on the alert for deception," said Paul Reynard.

"I hope I've convinced you," said Denise somewhat impatiently.

"Yes, you have." Paul Reynard smiled. "I am sure."

As he spoke, his hand came out of the desk drawer—with a gun. Then he pulled the bell rope.

"I am sure none of you will leave this chateau alive."

Chapter

15

A MINUTE AFTER Paul Reynard pulled the bell cord, his nephews ran into the room, guns drawn.

"You can put the guns away," Paul Reynard told them in a voice of curt command. "As you can see, I have the situation in control."

"Yes, sir," said Pierre, as he and his brothers obeyed. "I have to compliment you, sir. I never would have suspected Denise of being a police spy. It was brilliant of you to have set up this final test of her loyalty before we let her know you were the real boss."

"One can never be too careful—and one can trust nobody. I was sure that not even the most hardened police agent would let both these young Americans and a distinguished gentleman like me die without trying to save us. Denise proved that I was right, as usual."

"As *always,* sir," said Yves admiringly.

"I have not survived and prospered by making mistakes," added Paul Reynard.

"*You!* The master criminal! I can't believe it," exclaimed Denise, shaking her head. "You have a distinguished army career. The Legion of Honor. A noble name. *Why?*"

"As an intelligence officer in the Algerian War, I was ordered to break all rules in getting information from prisoners," explained Paul Reynard bitterly. "Then, after France lost that war, I was publicly given the Legion of Honor—and privately told that my military career was over as far as future promotions were concerned—because I had obeyed my orders too well. I saw then how foolish it was to be a patriot. I decided to live as my ancestors did, for myself and by my own rules." He paused and looked around, with a glow of triumph on his face. "I have created a kingdom where I alone rule—an international kingdom of crime."

As Denise and the Hardys stared at him in growing fear, he looked less like a king than an executioner.

"How did you want to dispose of them, sir?" asked Maurice. "Shall we bury them in the dungeon or in the garden?"

"You actually mean to kill us?" cried Denise, growing pale.

"You, an agent of the Sûreté, ask me *that?*" replied Paul Reynard contemptuously. "I am surprised at you. But I suppose that is only to be expected when the government hires females for such work. Such soft-minded thinking will be the ruin of France. In my day, we kept women out of dangerous situations. They would only fold under pressure, as you are doing right now, my dear young lady."

Denise *was* folding. She was pale as a ghost. She rubbed her fingers over her forehead, trying to wipe clear her mind. Then her hand dropped down, her mouth dropped open, and she dropped to the floor.

"Just like a woman to faint," said Paul Reynard, standing over her and looking down at her limp form.

He opened his mouth to say something else, but the words did not come out.

Instead there was only a grunt, as Denise's feet jackknifed up to kick him viciously in the gut.

Taken by surprise, the Reynard brothers hesitated—just an instant too long. Denise was on her feet, dashing for the door with Frank and Joe following.

Joe was the last out, slamming the door behind him—just in time. Bullets slammed into it. The nephews had recovered from their shock and drawn their guns.

Denise and the Hardys burst out of the house and raced across the grass to where the helicopter was parked, clearly illuminated by a giant full moon in the cloudless night sky.

They climbed into the chopper, Denise at the controls.

"Good thing Reynard fell for your trick," Frank said to Denise.

"Ah," said Denise. "I knew I could count on a Frenchman to believe in the weakness of women." She paused, looking down at the control board. "That does not mean that Paul Reynard is not a smart man."

"What do you mean?" asked Joe.

"He had the foresight to have the helicopter controls locked," said Denise. "We cannot take off."

"We'll have to run for it then," said Joe, already leaping out of the chopper. He hit the ground as a bullet whistled by his ear.

"We can do better than that," said Frank, as he and Denise jumped out, too. "Follow me."

Keeping their bodies low, the three ran for the stables while the night was filled with echoing gunshots.

Inside, Frank opened a stall and led out a splendid-looking stallion.

"Pick your mounts," said Frank. "Let's see what kind of racehorses these babies really are."

A moment later, Denise was astride a handsome gray horse. "I haven't ridden bareback in years, not since I was a little girl visiting my grandfather's farm."

"I've never ridden bareback, but now's a good

time to learn," said Frank, patting his horse's flank as he and the other mounts moved out of the stables.

"Come on, baby, let's make time." Joe gripped his horse tightly with his knees. He was bent over low with his face near the horse's mane and his arms wrapped around the animal's neck when the horse responded to the sound of another shot as if it were a starter's gun.

The horses streaked across the pasture. At the door in the wall surrounding the property, the three came to an abrupt halt.

Frank leaped off, unbolted it, swung it open, and remounted.

They were through it in an instant and racing down the moonlit asphalt road.

When they reached the highway, they stopped again.

"They must be in their car by now," said Frank. "You can be sure Paul Reynard has a fast one." He looked up and down the highway, surprised to see that it was empty. He glanced at his watch. It was three in the morning. "We can't beat them in a race. We'll have to outsmart them. They'll be expecting us to go to Bayeux. We'll go the other way. Come on."

The hoofbeats of the horses were thunderously loud as they pounded down the concrete highway. Joe had to yell to make himself heard over them.

"We've done it! We've shaken them!" he

shouted triumphantly, looking over his shoulder at the empty highway stretching behind them.

But his last words were drowned out by a loud sound, that was growing louder.

"They're using the helicopter!" cried Denise.

"Of course!" Frank shouted. He urged his horse to move still faster, the hoofbeats sounding like machine guns now. "I should have known! It's the perfect way to hunt us. They're high enough in the air to look down the road in both directions. The moon is as bright as a spotlight— they've probably seen us already."

At that moment, the three of them realized that they had to make another fast decision. In front of them, the highway came to an abrupt end, running into a road that cut it at right angles. The horses hesitated, not knowing which way to turn. The noise of the helicopter had become deafeningly close.

Frank looked up, then to the right, then to the left. "We'll go straight ahead!" he shouted. "Maybe we can find some cover in the countryside and lose them!"

The horses easily leaped the highway guardrails. They galloped up a low rise of land that was barren of trees and bushes, covered only with sparse grass.

Then they halted again.

They had reached the end of a cliff. Below, lit by moonlight, was a wide white beach and then the darkness of the sea.

"We have come to the English Channel," said Denise. "We cannot go any farther."

The noise of the helicopter grew still louder. It was descending.

"So these are the D-Day beaches," Frank mused. "The Allies staged the biggest invasion of all time here over forty years ago." Frank had always been a World War II buff, and the site of the Normandy landings had always filled him with fascination. For a moment he forgot the predicament he and the others were in. He sat motionless astride his horse and gazed down at the dimly lit glowing white sand as if hypnotized by its ghostly splendor, feeling the pull of the past like the pull of a tide out to sea.

"What a time for a history lesson," cried Joe in exasperation. He could see the helicopter now as it approached the ground less than a hundred feet away. In the moonlight, it looked like some prehistoric monster, its whirling blades starting to slow.

In seconds it would touch down. He could imagine the Reynards poised to jump out, their fingers on their triggers. "Hey, Frank! Unless we figure out what to do fast, *we'll* be history. This will be our D-Day, too. *Death day*."

Chapter

16

"WHERE CAN WE GO?" Denise cried desperately as the runners of the helicopter hit the ground and its door began to open.

"Nowhere on horseback, that's for sure," replied Frank. He jumped off his mount, and the others did the same.

"Here goes nothing! Let's hope the sand is soft," exclaimed Joe, as he reached the very edge of the bluff and prepared to leap. Then he saw that wasn't necessary. A path led downward. "Come on. Let's make tracks."

Struggling to keep their balance, the three scrambled down the narrow path. Ten feet from the bottom, the path ended, sheared away by wind erosion.

Without discussing the matter, all three of them jumped. They landed hard, sprawling on the sand. Almost instantly they were on their feet, brushing the sand off and looking upward.

The sound of the helicopter told them it had taken off again and was coming after them on the beach.

"Do you still have your gun, Denise?" Frank asked.

"Unfortunately, no," Denise answered. "Pierre asked me to give it to him right after you were locked in the dungeon. He claimed that Karl's was defective and that Karl needed a gun more than I did. I can see now that was just a way to disarm me before they tested me."

"Probably Paul Reynard's idea," said Frank. "He seems to think of everything."

"*We* have to think of something right now," said Joe. "That helicopter is coming down again."

"There is no way to climb back up the bluff," said Denise.

"The only thing we can do is split up and go in different directions," said Frank. "That way at least one of us might make it out of this alive."

They looked at each other solemnly for a moment.

Then Joe said to Denise, "Let me show you an American custom. We use it in basketball. It's called giving a high five."

"Right," said Frank, as he and his brother slapped each other's palms high in the air.

"I see!" said Denise, and the three of them did

it together. "Now I will show you a French custom," she said. Denise kissed Frank and Joe on both cheeks.

"Good luck," the three said at the same time.

And as the helicopter touched down on the beach they ran for their lives in three different directions.

Frank ran to the right, feet flying across the sand. His last sight of the others was Joe veering off to the left and Denise heading straight for the sea. None of them had any plan, which made Frank nervous. He didn't like to take things as they came.

As he ran, bullets whizzed past him. He was a moving target in the moonlight, and whoever was chasing him wouldn't keep missing those shots forever. All he could try was to run faster, faster.

Then it happened.

His foot sank into a hollow in the sand, and he fell to the ground face first. For a second he saw stars. Then his vision cleared, and he felt the pain shooting upward from his ankle. He didn't think it was a very bad sprain, but it was bad enough. His running speed was cut to a kind of limping hop. He was finished unless there was a miracle. And then he saw one.

It wasn't exactly a miracle, but it would do.

A squat shape rose ahead of him—some kind of building on the beach.

It took him only a minute to figure out what it was. He had seen pictures of structures like it in the same history books that had told him about the D-Day landing on this beach long ago.

It was a German pillbox—a squat cylindrical concrete fortress, big enough for three men and a machine gun. It hadn't been enough to stop the invasion, but it still stood, a monument to the odds that the invasion had overcome.

Ignoring the pain as he pushed himself to the limit, Frank made it through the entrance of the pillbox and stopped inside, panting.

At least he was still alive. He had bought himself about two minutes more time—until whoever was chasing him arrived at the pillbox. He knew he had been observed.

Frank moved away from the entrance to the old fortification, down five steps into the interior. The air was as cold and damp as the dungeon from which he had just escaped, as cold and damp as a tomb. He shivered. His groping hand touched cold concrete. He had retreated as far as he could. He was trapped. Frank could only wait for his enemy to enter and finish him off like an animal penned up for slaughter.

He smiled ironically. This must have been how the German soldiers in the pillbox felt as they crouched here, after their guns had failed to drive off the invading Allied forces. They must have waited, knowing their enemies could encircle their position and at any moment charge in, blocking all chance of escape.

Or maybe the Germans had thought of that when they built this, Frank thought.

They must have.

Frantically he felt along the concrete wall until he found the opening to an emergency exit on the side.

"I hope it's not blocked up with sand after all these years," he said to himself as he entered a tunnel that was just big enough for a man to crawl through.

A minute later, he felt the fresh air on his face, and then saw the moon, still enormous in the sky. It was the most beautiful thing he had ever seen.

But he did not pause to admire it. He had to move fast—as fast as he could on his hands and knees in the sand—before his pursuer realized he had gotten out.

Frank didn't plan to run away, though. His ankle hurt too much. He wouldn't get far enough. Besides, what he really wanted to do was attack.

He slipped silently around the side of the pill-box and found himself looking at Pierre's back.

Pierre was peering into the pillbox with his gun drawn.

"Come out, American," Pierre's taunting voice called into the darkness. "You do not have a chance. We have already caught your friends. Would you not like to see them one last time before you—"

That was as far as Pierre got. Frank delivered a

powerful karate chop that scored a dead hit on a key nerve in the back of Pierre's neck. Pierre went down without a fight.

Frank didn't waste time bothering to check him out. He grabbed Pierre's gun and headed back up the beach. Maybe Pierre had been lying when he claimed that Joe and Denise had been captured. Or if it was true, maybe Frank could come to their rescue.

At any rate, with a gun in his hand and Pierre out of the way, the odds for survival had become a whole lot better.

The odds for survival didn't look good for Joe as he ran down the beach away from Frank and Denise. He was moving as if he were in a broken-field run during a football game. But this time there was no goal line where he could stop and be safe. And bullets were harder to dodge than any tackler who had ever come after him.

The sand began to grow into a ridge ahead of him, sloping up more and more steeply into a respectable sand dune. Joe slogged uphill, losing speed, while his pursuer, still on level ground, drew nearer.

Joe pushed himself harder as the dune grew steeper, pulling with his hands as well as pushing with his legs. The top of the dune was almost in reach. He grabbed a clump of coarse dune grass. He'd be over it in another second, momentarily safe. And beyond . . . As his head cleared the crest, he saw a shape farther along the beach. A boat?

Behind him a shot rang out, and the clump of grass under his hand disintegrated as the bullet tore through it. A near miss—but it had killed him as surely as if it had hit him in the heart. Without a handhold, he couldn't climb over the dune. And his handhold had just been blasted apart. Joe scrabbled desperately for another clump of grass, but his hands only caught sand as he slipped a foot, then two feet down the slope.

Joe glanced back, and his heart sank. He was trapped on the empty dune, like a fly on a table-cloth. Below him, at the foot of the dune, his pursuer went down on one knee, bracing himself for the final shot.

If only I had a weapon, Joe thought, even something to throw at him, a stone. But there was nothing to throw, except his own body.

Sliding farther down the slope, Joe got his legs under him, then sprang into the air.

Caught by surprise, the gunman below rose to his feet, trying to bring his pistol up. By then Joe's feet were connecting with the man's shoulder, sending the gun flying and both of them rolling to the ground.

Fiercely they wrestled in the sand, grunting, sweating, hunting for a winning hold. The power-ful arms of his opponent closed around him in a crushing bear hug. Joe went limp. Then with sudden, violent motion of both arms, he broke free, throwing his opponent to the sand.

Joe rose up on his knees, drawing back his fist. Before the stunned Frenchman could move, Joe delivered the knockout punch—right on the guy's chin. It might have bruised Joe's knuckles, but as he got to his feet, he could be sure his opponent wouldn't be getting up for a good long time.

Joe squinted in the moonlight, trying to see whom he had attacked. It was Yves Reynard. Then Joe turned to hunt for Yves's gun, but before he could find it, he saw another figure running toward him. He turned, charging back to the top of the sand dune, then dashing for the only cover in sight—a large rowboat beached upside down a hundred yards away. Joe stayed low as he ran, expecting shots as soon as his pursuer cleared the dune.

Not a shot was fired, though. Maybe he hadn't been spotted after all. Joe crouched behind the boat, his ears picking up the faint crunching sound of approaching footsteps in the sand.

The footsteps drew closer and closer—and Joe leaped up, his fist already swinging in a hay-maker.

But even as he threw the punch, Joe's target ducked and grabbed his arm. Suddenly Joe was flying through the air, to land face forward in the sand.

Instantly he was on his feet, ready to swing

again, when Frank said, "Hey, it's me! I came to help you, but I see you've done a pretty good job by yourself, even with your primitive fighting techniques."

"Did you overpower that other guy?" asked Joe.

"Yup," said Frank. "But we don't have time to stand around congratulating ourselves."

"Yeah, we have to save Denise," said Joe.

But they were stopped before they could take a step.

Facing them, five feet away, was Maurice Reynard, his gun leveled.

"Drop your gun," Maurice ordered Frank, and Frank had to obey.

"You two were clever, but not clever enough. Now back off from the boat, in case you have any idea of diving for cover."

Frank and Joe exchanged helpless glances. They had no choice but to obey.

Smiling, Maurice stood between them and the boat. "That is the end of your bag of tricks. Uncle Paul said that he preferred that we bring you back to be tortured so that you would reveal your secrets. But he said we could kill you if necessary. I have decided—"

At that moment, Maurice's gun fell from his hand as the blade of an oar smashed across the back of his head. Then his body collapsed in the sand, covering the gun.

Denise dropped the oar she had swung and was

on her hands and knees instantly, rolling Maurice over to get her hands on the gun.

Before the Hardys' startled eyes, she had emerged from under the boat with the oar in her hands. It had been all they could do to keep their faces straight.

"Good job," Frank congratulated her.

"As you Americans say, no sweat." Denise got to her feet with the gun.

"*No* sweat?" said Joe, looking at her soaked clothing.

"Oh, *that*," replied Denise. "I merely took a little swim. I jumped into the sea, swam underwater, and while the Reynards were looking in the area where they'd seen me go under, I rode the breakers in farther down the beach. I saw this boat lying here and crawled under it."

"Undercover work is definitely your specialty," said Joe, grinning.

"I do my best." Denise smiled. "And you two don't do so badly either."

"Three down, one to go," said Frank. "Let's take the helicopter back to the chateau before Paul Reynard starts worrying that something has gone wrong."

"And his nephews?" asked Joe.

"Denise can alert the police to pick them up anytime," replied Frank. "But Paul Reynard will be harder to handle if he makes a run for it."

Frank picked up the gun he had dropped. Joe went back to the dune and found Yves's gun.

Then they headed toward the helicopter, which was parked on the beach.

"I can't wait to see the expression on old Uncle Paul's face when he sees us," said Joe as they reached the helicopter and Joe's hand reached out to open the door.

But the door flew open before he touched it.

Paul Reynard stood there with a gun in his hand, an evil look of triumph on his face.

"You have had your fun," he said, waving Joe back with his gun. Then he climbed out of the helicopter. "But now your fun is over. Now it is my turn. As you Americans say, he who laughs last, laughs best.

"You actually thought you could outsmart me," he went on. "You should have known that I would be thinking one step ahead of every move you made. Now at last your luck has run out. March—to your deaths."

Chapter
17

REYNARD GESTURED WITH his gun for Denise, Frank, and Joe to march ahead of him down the beach. Silently they obeyed. As they walked along, Paul Reynard spoke boastfully to them, enjoying his triumph to the fullest.

"I could, of course, kill you this very second with three quick bullets," he said. "I assure you, that is all it would take. I am an excellent shot, and I have the pistol championship medals to prove it. I would have no trouble putting a bullet in each of your brains at this short distance.

"But that would end our game far too quickly. Such a short, sweet death would not be punishment enough for the trouble you have caused me. It would rob me of the pleasure of seeing you tremble with terror and sweat with fear. It would be like making a meal of fast food, instead of dining properly, as a good Frenchman should, savoring each well-prepared morsel of the feast. Now march up this trail."

Again the three of them had to obey. They hiked up a trail that led from the beach to a patch of high ground directly overlooking the sea. Frank noticed another old German gun emplacement, but before he could make a move toward it, Paul Reynard said, "Do not even think of ducking into that shelter. You would die before you took two steps. Just continue walking until I tell you to stop."

Their march became a climb as the cliff top rose higher, then higher still. Soon they stood looking down at the moonlit sea far below.

"You may turn to face me," said Paul Reynard.

They did so, and saw him standing ten feet away, his gun leveled at them.

"Observe how elegant your execution will be," he said. "My bullets will hit you and you will drop off the edge of the cliff into the sea below. Perhaps the tides will wash you out so that you will never be found. It doesn't matter, though. There will be nothing in the world to link me with your deaths."

Joe could stand it no longer. "Look, do me a favor and just blow me away, instead of boring me to death with your speeches," he said angrily.

"You Reynards seem better at shooting off your mouths than your guns."

Anger shadowed Paul Reynard's face as well.

"So you find me boring," he snarled. "Before you go to sleep, let me wake you up by showing you what this gun will soon do to you—and what kind of terror you should feel."

Rage gleaming in his eyes, Paul Reynard pointed his gun at the ground to demonstrate its deadly power. He pulled the trigger. There was a deafening report as the gun went off.

And then there was an even louder explosion, an explosion that hurled Paul Reynard backward, his gun hand instinctively shielding his face.

Denise, Frank, and Joe didn't have to look at each other to know what to do. Instantly they attacked.

Frank hit Reynard high, Joe hit him low, and Denise snatched up his gun from where it had fallen.

She trained it on him as he sat on the ground, still half-stunned, shaking his head in bewilderment.

"What happened?" he asked hoarsely.

Denise read a large sign that was posted on the area where they stood: "Warning: Unexploded shells and mines. Do not enter upon penalty of the law."

Frank grinned at Reynard.

"This was a bad place to go shooting off your

gun," Frank said. "Now you see what happens when you break the law."

His joke wasn't very good, but that didn't stop the three of them from laughing at it.

Two days later, flight bookings and customs and passport clearances had been arranged for the Hardy brothers. With the Reynards finished and the Hardys out of danger, the Network was only too willing to help.

"Good thing you remembered the Gray Man's temporary number," Joe had said to Frank.

"Elementary, my good man," Frank had replied, smiling.

"At least the Gray Man was happy to see us," Joe said.

"I think he was happier to see that hundred and fifty thousand dollars," Frank replied.

The smiles that the Hardys exchanged with Denise were somewhat rueful, more notably Joe's.

"I'd really like to see you again," he told Denise as they stood saying goodbye at the departure gate of the airport. "Especially without my brother hanging around. You know what they say about two being company."

"Come on, Joe," said Frank. "Denise has already told you she's really twenty-five. That's why the Sûreté gave her the assignment. She's so young looking."

"I have nothing against older women," replied Joe. "In fact, for a man of the world like me, girls my own age are, well, just girls."

"I'm sure the girls back in Bayport will be interested in hearing that," said Frank. "You'll tell them, of course."

"I would, except I don't want to blow my cover. But Denise, you know the real me: I'm a man of action, much older than my years. Maybe we can work together again sometime."

"I hope so," said Denise with a smile. "And now, I have to say goodbye to you. There's still so much work to be done, tying up the loose ends of Reynard and Company, arresting all the people they used. It will keep me busy for months. But after that, who knows what the future may hold?"

With that, she said goodbye to both Hardys in the French style, placing warm kisses on their cheeks.

"So tell me, Joe," Frank said, grinning. "Do you think French women are something special?"

"I don't care what country she comes from. *That* woman is special," Joe said, gazing after Denise as she walked briskly through the crowd at the air terminal.

"Come on, we have a plane to catch," said Frank. "It's time to go back to the real world."

"You know, the more we operate in the

Network's world, the more trouble I have knowing which is real—the nice safe world we live in most of the time, or the one the Network shows us," remarked Joe, as they walked through the departure gate.

"It is pretty weird sometimes," agreed Frank. "Makes me feel like I'm a split personality."

"But you have to admit, it keeps things from getting dull," added Joe.

"I won't argue with that. But all I want now is a nice dull trip home. And before that, I want to have my old dull clothes and my old dull hair back again."

That wasn't so easy, though. At least, the hair wasn't easy.

After the Hardys arrived in New York, they immediately returned to the punk hairdresser who had given them their haircuts and dye jobs. When she examined their hair, she shook her rainbow-colored head.

"This isn't *my* work," she said indignantly.

"We, er, had to have a few changes made," said Frank.

"Well, you should have come back to me," the young woman said.

"Believe me, if we could have, we would have," said Joe with his most winning smile.

"Well, you'll have to wait a long time for your natural hair to grow in," she said.

"What do you mean?" asked Frank.

"I mean that the dye job I gave you could be washed out when you were finished with it," said the hairdresser. "But whoever did this job did it for keeps."

"Ouch," said Frank, wincing. "This is *just* the way to come back from a New York vacation. Dad may have a few questions, though."

"I think my dating prospects for the year have just turned to zero," said Joe.

"Wait a minute," Frank said. "Couldn't you dye our hair back to its original color? He's blond, and I have brown hair."

"Well, I've never tried anything like that before, I mean using ordinary colors like *blond* and *brown*. But it would be a challenge."

Two hours later, after the hairdresser finished her work, the Hardys were enormously grateful.

"You're welcome, I'm sure," she said. "But I must say, I feel as if I've betrayed my art. Blond and brown. I mean, that's simply not where it's at."

"But that's where we're going to," said Joe. "Home, to ordinary Bayport."

As they climbed into the taxi that would take them to Grand Central Station, Frank glanced at himself and his brother in the rearview mirror. "She did a good job," he said. "But it does feel funny, disguising ourselves as ourselves."

"Yeah, it makes me wonder who we really are," said Joe. "Two ordinary young Americans or a high-risk international crime-fighting team."

"I guess we're both," replied Frank.

"And I guess I like that combination just fine," said Joe, already looking forward to the future and their next adventure.

Frank and Joe's next case:

The Hardy boys attempt the daring rescue of their friend Holly Strang, who has fallen into the clutches of the Rajah, a sinister cult leader. And when the Rajah captures Frank, he tries every mind-twisting trick to convert him, too.

With all the odds against them, the Hardys just barely escape with Holly. Now they must survive a terrifying chase through rugged terrain, with the Rajah's fanatical followers on their trail. But the worst danger is much closer—a human time bomb, programmed to kill at the Rajah's orders!

Can Frank and Joe break the Rajah's twisted web of power? Find out in *Cult of Crime*, Case #3 in The Hardy Boys Casefiles.

HAVE YOU SEEN THE HARDY BOYS® LATELY?